TOTAL ECLIPSE

O dark, dark, dark amid the blaze of noon,
Irrecoverably dark, total eclipse
Without all hope of day!

  —Milton, Samson Agonistes

TOTAL ECLIPSE

John Brunner

Science Fiction

WEIDENFELD AND NICOLSON
LONDON

© Brunner Fact and Fiction Ltd

First published in Great Britain in 1975 by
Weidenfeld and Nicolson
11 St John's Hill London SW11

ISBN 0 297 77006 3

Printed in Great Britain by
Redwood Burn Limited
Trowbridge & Esher

I

. . . and there it is!

Brilliant as a blob of quicksilver it shone on the grey-chalk oblate of the planet's moon: a jewel amid a ruin of decay. From this distance, thousands of kilometres away, it was minuscule. No details could be made out such as were to be discerned in the pictures they had all studied at home on Earth.

Nonetheless, to see it in real time was very different from looking at photographs. It was right to plot the course for *Stellaris,* between her emergence from qua-space and her approach to a landing on Sigma Draconis III, so that for these few minutes the light of the local star would glint off that incredible artefact and waken in the minds of those arriving here for the first time an echo of the shock experienced by the explorers who had chanced on it back in 2020, on what otherwise would almost certainly have been the last of man's attempts to visit the stars in view of the disappointments of Proxima, Epsilon Eridani and Tau Ceti—or at any rate the last in the foreseeable future.

But of course finding that thing . . . !

A shiver crawled down Ian Macauley's spine. A curl of his untidy red hair, bending over to touch his freckled forehead, felt like a ghostly alien caress, and he shot up his hand to brush it aside. Against his will—no, more exactly: without conscious intention— he found himself reciting dry statistics under his breath.

Diameter thirty-six point oh five kilometres. Wall height one point one nine kilometres averaged. Thickness of the mirror—

With an effort he cut short the recital of bare stark figures and switched to words, which he cared for a great deal more:

They, whoever, whatever they were, came to their moon and smoothed and rounded and polished a whole vast crater and made it into the largest telescope imaginable. And they're dead. They've been dead for a hundred thousand years. Yet the first trace we can find of them was only three thousand years earlier; it's as though the weight of a thousand centuries has compressed the whole of their history—come to that, the whole of their evolution—into a layer no thicker than a little seam of coal, memorial to the sprouting, heyday and downfall of a million trees!

In spite of which, should they so choose, these latecomers, these humans from Earth, could wipe away the meteoritic dust which had accumulated on the mirror of the telescope, and mend half a dozen breaches caused by larger-than-usual chunks of cosmic garbage, and substitute their own inanimate electronics for the—the whatevers that its builders had employed, long desiccated into incomprehensible black shreds . . . and the telescope would still be usable.

"It's unbelievable!"

He had not meant to speak aloud, nor did he realise he had done so until a caustic voice from behind him said, "Yes, I'm sure it is. But I'd like a glimpse of it, too, *please!*"

Hastily he stepped aside from the viewport, muttering apologies and a trifle relieved that his successor was no one other than plump, plain, likable Karen Vlady, the civil engineer among their party.

She had been the first of his companions to whom he had spoken directly. On the day of his arrival at the Sigma Draconis Briefing Centre in Canberra, Australia, he had been horribly frightened; he was still scarcely able to believe either that the famous Igor Andrevski, the chief archeologist out here, had asked for him by name, or that he had had the courage to say yes.

Though I should have realised I had no need to worry, shouldn't I? The prospect of being cooped up in the ship like this felt dreadfully daunting, yet everything has gone very pleasantly . . . or almost everything. And during my stay here I may in some ways be better off than I'd have been at home: one of thirty people whom anybody would be proud to call a friend, brilliant handpicked experts among whom I can expect to feel instantly at ease. On Earth, in a city or even at a university, they'd be diluted among thousands of other people who might be boring, or annoying, or a nuisance!

He was by temperament a solitary man, but if he had to live in close proximity with others, these were exactly the sort he would have chosen. It was that point which his first encounter with Karen had started to make plain to him.

She had heard him muttering his name as he presented himself at the centre's reception desk, and come up to him and said with characteristic forthrightness, "So you're Ian Macauley, are you? What's it like to live inside your head?"

Taken aback by the directness of the question, he had replied, "Oh . . . ! Think of a haunted house!"

Which was something he had occasionally confided to intimates, but never before to a perfect stranger.

A couple more of his then-unknown colleagues had been in earshot, and mistaken his answer for a flip joke. So the first impression he'd made on them was that he had a dry sense of humour. But Karen had not missed the crucial fact: the statement was literal. He appreciated that.

So now he was actually here, the best part of nineteen light-years from the solar system, to take his turn at wrestling with a riddle that had defied Earth's finest thinkers for the best part of a decade.

It's a crazy paradox, that we should know so much about them, and so little! We know, roughly, what they looked like—bodies like two matching crab shells one above the other, four short walking limbs, two grasping limbs, all tipped with tubular claws down which ran nerve channels, and composed of a modified version of their hidelike skin, as are human nails. We know, or think we know, that they were possessed of a sense we don't have, though many fishes do: the ability to perceive electromagnetic fields. We suspect the many crystals we've found still impregnated with such fields, after the manner of a tape recording, were their counterpart of inscriptions. Which is why I'm here. Conversely, they seem to have lacked means to detect sound, barring perhaps the very loudest and coarsest. We know they had a high science, which argues

*a complex culture, also evidenced by their quite large city-sites—but
why are there not many more of those? Certain hints suggest they
had a religion, or religions; maybe, for all we can tell, they had
the equivalents of poetry and music, expressed in terms of infinitely
subtle electrical fields. What can it have been like to live in a world
without sound, but where your whole being resonated to the ebb
and flow, the very heartbeat, of the planet and all the creatures on
it?*

He clenched his fists, forcing his nails deep into his palms.

*How can I make myself comprehend the utter nonhumanity of
those who built that telescope? Because if I don't succeed in that,
my visit, and all the agonies of doubt I sweated through before
deciding to accept the invitation, and at least three, possibly five
years of my life, will be completely wasted. Oh, how I'd hate to be
rotated home and leave the mystery unsolved—how I pity those
who thirty days from now will face that fate! The only thing worse
will be if it turns out they've solved the problem in the last two
years!*

There were three viewports in the control cabin of the *Stellaris*.
During most of each voyage they were irrelevant. In qua-space
there was no energy propagation in any form human eyes could
detect. But it was worth having them. The designers had been put
to immense trouble to compensate for the stresses they induced in
the hull; extra struts and girders had had to be included which
increased the vessel's dry mass by over 4 per cent . . . but for the
privilege of seeing, at the beginning and end of each journey, the
naked universe with the naked eye instead of solely via TV relays,
it was a negligible price to pay.

That, at any rate, was the opinion of her commander, Colonel
Rudolf Weil.

The *Stellaris*'s crew likewise numbered three, and during most
of each voyage they were as irrelevant as the viewports. No human
being could hope to match the nanosecond reflexes involved in
making a Big Step between the stars. Above all, it took machines
to ensure that when it was time to dissipate the phenomenal energy
acquired on the way to hyperphotonic velocities there was nothing

in the ship's path of emergence larger than a grain of dust. Even so, no matter what exit angle was chosen, there were always solar flares and minor perturbations in the orbits of local asteroids and comets.

He had sometimes mentioned to close friends a dream that haunted him concerning the disappearance of the Draconians: the possibility that they had been less lucky than mankind when they made their first experiments with hyperdrive. He knew, intellectually, that if the reason for the aliens' extinction were to be found in some unlooked-for side effect of flying a ship faster than light—as, for instance, a destabilisation of the sun—evidence to prove it would have been found by now, printed in moonrock as though in a block of photographic emulsion. And there was no evidence; there were very nearly no clues. Yet the dream recurred, over and over.

Right from the beginning humans had been cautious about quaspace. It wasn't only a matter of trespassing into a mode of existence which all the classic theories regarded as forbidden. Theories could be scrapped, and inevitably were, on the day when a tiny five-ton package of instruments arrived in moon orbit a detectable fraction of a second ahead of the signal saying it had been dispatched from Earth orbit.

More to the point, beyond doubt, was the fact that it had been so damnably *expensive* to build the starship. The planet Earth possessed exactly one interstellar craft, and this was it, and it strained mankind's resources to the utmost to send her out and back once every two years across what by galactic standards amounted to a tiny little distance.

Maybe that was the sort of thing that handicapped the aliens, but it hit them sooner. I remember last time Valentine Rorschach was asking why we've found just one of so many things: one wrecked and sunken oceangoing ship, one large flying machine, one and only one of many thousands of types of artefact. . . . But of course so much of their civilisation lies buried under sediment and peat and avalanches that had it not been for the telescope we'd never have suspected its existence.

Watching the passengers as they lined up to take their turn at the viewport currently facing the moon, he felt a tremor pass through him, recalling how shaken he had been at his own first sight of that brilliant spark. Then he had been only a captain—not that rank mattered much when it came to doing something that had never been done before. In those days *Stellaris* had been commanded by Rear Admiral Boris Ivanov, but he had had to retire after that trip; there was too loud a murmur in his heart valves. Some people had suggested the ship be converted to crewless operation; there was no theoretical reason why it should not be launched and landed automatically. But it remained true that no machine could deal with the passengers' problems, let alone the question of whether people wanted to be shot from star to star like dead packages. So there were still crew in charge.

How do these passengers really regard me, the ferryman—the Charon who may have conveyed them on their last voyage? There have already been two deaths here, on this alien planet. We may be about to learn of more.

For himself, there would certainly never be another Big Step after the homeward leg of this trip. He had grown prematurely old, thanks to the radiation of space; his round face was seamed with wrinkles like a shrunken apple, and there was more grey than brown in his hair. If the *Stellaris* did come back, even if only to evacuate the planet, he would not be her commander.

By rights, his successor ought to be Captain Irene Bakongu, the older, the more experienced, the senior of his companions.

The way things are going back on Earth, though, that may not count. A shame, because if it's going to be done at all—which is by no means certain—it should be done properly.

And because Irene was both female and black, the choice was more likely to fall on Lieutenant Gyorgy Somogyi.

Who's less well qualified and far less quick-thinking. High on the list of possible explanations for the extinction of the Draconians, so they tell me, is the idea that it was due to some fundamental flaw in their nature. All too easily some stupid irrational prejudice could get rid of us, too, couldn't it? Thinking of which . . .

It dawned on him that only nine of their ten passengers were present, and before he could stop himself he had asked aloud, turning to Irene: "What's happened to the general?"

At which there were visible shudders from everybody and a moment of frozen silence, broken by a hateful rasping voice from the doorway of the control cabin.

"Were you referring to me by any chance . . . *Colonel?*"

II

Not wanting to obstruct anybody else waiting for a precious, perhaps never-to-be-repeated sight of the alien telescope, Ian had withdrawn from the viewport, threading his way between the three control chairs and the close-packed bodies of his companions, and taken station right beside the doorway. Now he withdrew a fraction further still: into himself.

I guess it's a sick comment on humanity that the thing which binds me most closely to these comparative strangers, crew included, is not shared interests but shared detestation. We all loathe this horrible bastard!

But he did his best to maintain the formalities and gave a polite nod as the latecomer pushed past: General José Maria Ordoñez-Vico, small and neat and dapper with a tiny black moustache, a bachelor aged forty-eight, the sole person aboard or indeed ever transported by the *Stellaris* who had declined the plain practical clothing traditionally worn in space—a zip-fronted blouse with big pockets, loose comfortable pants, and elastic sandals over which spacegear could be drawn in emergency—and insisted on sporting his military uniform complete with rank badges, medal ribbons, and epaulettes. When Karen had relayed to Ian a rumour that the general had only with difficulty been dissuaded from bringing his ceremonial sword, he had simply chuckled, assuming it to be a happy invention. Now, after thirty days in space with him, he was prepared to believe the charge was true.

Paradoxically, however, if this man had not been allowed to displace someone more valuable, the *Stellaris* would never have been launched on this trip . . . and the thirty people currently on Sigma Draconis III might have been abandoned to struggle on alone. And no doubt die out as completely as the natives.

Well—we think there are thirty people here. By now there may be fewer. . . . In an upside-down way, that may be an advantage. Ten members of the base staff, presumably, have been preparing themselves to be rotated home. There will only be space for nine after all . . . that is, unless he orders the closure of the base, and on her last-ever Big Step the Stellaris *carries a record complement of forty-three. And leaves everything behind except their food, their water and their air.*

The reason for Ordoñez-Vico's presence was, in Ian's view, terrifyingly typical of just such a flaw in the nature of mankind as was now suspected of having betrayed the species which long ago had travelled from Sigma Draconis III to the local moon . . . and apparently no farther.

He was the commander in chief of the Bolivian Military Intelligence Service.

From the first moment starflight was found to be possible it had been obvious that the resources of only the very richest nations could support a faster-than-light ship. To build the first ocean liners strained the then-wealthiest countries; to operate international airlines was at first the privilege of the fortunate few . . . and building the planes to provide them remained for decades a near monopoly; to land humans on the moon was, also for decades, the unique accomplishment of the nation that could afford the computers to back up the astronauts, the precision engineering skills which reached the point where 99.99 per cent reliability would have resulted in about fifteen thousand things going wrong and the wastage inherent in training dozens of reserve personnel at enormous cost for the sake of being certain that on the day of the chosen launch-window at least one crew would be intact.

It would just about—just barely—have been possible for one country to build and fly a small starship: perhaps with a crew of four and minimal equipment. It would also have been within the compass of a consolidated cluster like Common Europe or the leader of a loose economic alliance like Japan.

But it would have been very, very unpopular to do that. Articulate, indeed vociferous, the citizens of less fortunate countries had long been objecting to the way a pyramid of glorious achievement was casually built on a foundation of human rubble. The eagle-keen eye of a billion-dollar satellite might look down on the corpse of a labourer who had dug ore for it on starvation wages, and was dead.

Nonetheless, the situation had improved considerably since the last worldwide recession. The climate was right for some grand gesture. So the idea dawned with all the brilliance of the first sunrise following an Arctic winter:

Why not a U.N. Starflight Fund, to which each country would contribute in strict proportion to its GNP?

The suggestion was eventually approved, and the designers of the projected ship heaved a sigh of relief and stopped worrying about cutting everything to the bone. The funds voted were enough to finance a ship with three crew and well over a hundred tons of nonpermanent mass—a jargon phrase meaning cargo and/or passengers with the means to support them.

Three years building and testing led to three years of disappointing, fruitless expeditions to barren systems that added much to the store of abstract knowledge, nothing to the rapidly dwindling resources of overpopulated, seething Earth.

The cost mounted. Each trip pointed the way to refinements and modifications; each caused some trifling damage, so that one "might as well" incorporate an improvement as simply repair the faulty components . . . and each time the improvement cost more, called for subtler techniques, laid a heavier burden on the Starflight Fund.

People began to ask, "Why bother?" And there was no good answer—until the last grand fling, the shot to a star more distant than before but resembling Earth's sun more nearly than its predecessors, revealed the terrifying fact symbolised by the incredible telescope.

There had been a high civilisation at Sigma Draconis.

It too had achieved spaceflight.

And it was gone. Vanished. Disappeared.

Whence the fearful, haunting question: *Is the same likely to happen to us?*

The immediate impact of the news was predictable. A special levy was raised for the Starflight Fund. Ten carefully chosen experts, together with the most compact and most advanced equipment both to keep them alive and to conduct research with on arrival, were hurriedly flown to the mystery planet.

The sense of alarm endured long enough to finance another visit, and another, and by the skin of humanity's teeth, another yet. This was, to be precise, the fifth expedition. The first had been exploratory, in 2020; the next landed the nucleus of a permanent ground staff in 2022; the staff had been added to, ten at a time, in 2024 and 2026; now it was 2028 and this was the first rotation trip, the first time people who had been—who had survived—here since 2022 were due to be taken home.

But the trip was unique in another way, too. Never before had the ship been late. And it might become unique in still another respect, with the discontinuation of the base. It was not exactly in the lap of the gods, that . . . not unless there was a god called Ordoñez-Vico.

The apprehension had diminished. The sense of frustration had grown, as the third and fourth expeditions reported no progress. And then, all too typically . . .

There had been famine in half a dozen densely populated countries, all of whose governments were controlled by greedy, short-sighted, thoughtless men whose first reaction when the starving mobs came battering at their gates was to accuse a scapegoat. The Starflight Fund was an obvious target. Rumours took their rise: *here's another way the rich are cheating the poor, for if you hadn't had to subsidise the fund, there'd be another million in the treasury to spend on food!*

No mention, of course, of the fact that the Prime Minister had made his fortune by hoarding rice during the previous famine, or that the President's brother owned the nation's largest pharmaceutical factory and was taking a profit of 1700 per cent on every ampul of niacin, ascorbic acid and B_{12}. That news was stale.

And then another, different, more dangerous story began to spread:

Out there they've found the weapons that killed the native race. They're coming back to threaten you with them—they're coming back to rule the world!

How anybody, no matter how ignorant, could take that seriously was a question that defeated Ian, let alone the problem of how sophisticated delegates to the United Nations could refer to it in their speeches and not burst out laughing. Still, it had happened . . . and that was why General Ordoñez-Vico had been given power to order the abandonment of the Draco base, and the abolition of the Starflight Fund, if any hint, clue, trifling suspicion, triggered his all too obvious latent paranoia.

And here he was, scowling as usual at Captain Bakongu whom he made no secret of hating both as a person and as a symbol— hailing as he did from an elitist, racialist, masculinist background— and saying to Colonel Weil, "Tell me something! Does this detour you're making, like the pilot of an airliner bound for Rio who wants to show off the Sugarloaf, form part of your prescribed schedule?"

There was electric tension in the filtered, processed air. But Weil's answer was perfectly polite . . . at first.

"Yes, General, it's a regular feature of our visits. In fact"—and here malice stalked in, a twist of his voice, as it were—"I'm surprised to hear you ask. I gathered that you'd made an exhaustive study of the records from all our trips."

Ordoñez-Vico responded in a manner they were all familiar with. He drew from his jacket a flat object, little larger than an old-fashioned pocket watch though a great deal heavier and square instead of round, and consulted the dials on its face with an important air.

It was, so the general had repeatedly declared, the most advanced lie detector ever devised, capable of catching out untruths by comparing the sonic profile of the speaker's words with his or her bodily secretions. During the thirty days since they left Earth hardly one conversation with him—not that there were many all told—had been completed without this gadget being produced for examination.

"It's not unknown for records to be falsified," Ordoñez-Vico said. "But I am relieved to note that on this occasion you are telling the truth." He repocketed the device. "Very well. I too require to see the vaunted telescope left behind by the alleged native species."

At that everyone else in the cabin gasped: a wordless chorus of incredulity.

"You honestly think somebody invented the Draconians?" a voice blurted . . . and, as all eyes turned on him, Ian blushed almost as red as his carroty hair. Weil repressed a chuckle. Most of his passengers this time, like most of those on earlier voyages, were academic types, accustomed to the formal hierarchical environment of a university. Ian was a refreshing contrast. He had spent most of his career burrowing into the ground at remote archeological sites, or sitting up late alone in an isolated forest hut, refusing to see or speak to anybody as he reinvented from first principles the reasons why, in a long-lost civilisation, people had chosen *this* rather than any other symbol to convey *that* of all possible meanings.

If only he were not so shy . . . Of all the people I've Charoned here, I'd put my money on Ian to unravel this mystery. I'd have liked to get to know him a lot better.

But there were other and more immediate problems on Weil's mind. He said crisply, "General, there is nothing alleged about the Draconians. They did reach their moon; they did build their scope; they did disappear! It will give me great personal pleasure to walk you around some of the sites that have been discovered and hear your version of how they were faked!"

He put an infinitesimal stress on the word *walk,* and there were discreet smiles on several faces. Ordoñez-Vico wore the softest and most delicate style of shoes. It was hard to picture him on an army route-march or up to his knees in a swamp.

But the irony was lost on him. He said, "I shall indeed accompany you, Colonel. I don't intend to let you do anything on this planet without my knowledge." And appended with a glower at the rest of the passengers: "Nor any of you, either!"

What might have flared in seconds into a blazing row was fore-stalled by a faint, faint sound from the communications panel and a sharp exclamation from Lieutenant Somogyi who was sitting be-fore it with earphones on.

"Colonel, we have voice contact with the base, and they're asking why we're so late."

"Don't answer that!" Ordoñez-Vico barked. "Do no more than acknowledge!"

Somogyi—still under thirty, making only his second trip, en-gagingly youthful in many respects despite the sinister cast of his gypsylike features and his undeniably formidable intellect—looked blank, and thereby tempted the general into explanations.

"I want to catch them before they have a chance to cover up what they're really doing!"

"In that case"—prompt from Captain Bakongu at the navigation panel—"all passengers should go immediately to strap-down sta-tions. If we line up for an approach now, we can save a full braking orbit. We could be down in about forty-four minutes."

"There's your chance," Weil said dryly. "Return to your cabins quickly, please."

Fury and the urge to appear consistent struggled in Ordoñez-Vico's face, but after a few seconds he swallowed his annoyance and gave a nod.

"Yes, Colonel. You are correct; we should make our landing right away."

And when the passengers had gone, escorted by Irene, Weil said more to the bulkheads than to Somogyi, "I wouldn't care to set the record he's about to: being the first man hated by literally every-one else on a whole damn' planet!"

III

After the shock of finding the telescope, the first human visitors had judged it politic to do nothing whatever to offend its builders. Though they could spot no lighted cities on the night side of the planet, that meant nothing; the natives might have evolved beyond the need for them, or bypassed it. There was nothing but stellar static on the radio bands, but that was equally irrelevant; there might be long-distance communications techniques humans had not yet discovered. And at first glance it had been plain that the telescope was very, very old.

Weil, the junior member of the crew on that particular voyage, had snapped at a persistent reporter after his return, "Damn it, we expected to meet them, remember! For all we knew it could have been like sailing the *Pinta* into Greater Hamburg!"

Which would have made a telling point but for the fact that the reporter was from Singapore and had not been exposed in school to the details of Columbus's explorations. He asked how to spell *Pinta*, consulted his portable reference computer, and inquired with no discernible trace of embarrassment what a twentieth-century sales slogan coined by the British Milk Marketing Board had to do with interstellar travel.

Anyhow: it was obvious at once that this world's ecology must be similar to Earth's, and that obligated the crew to sterilise their landing site. The only possible spot to touch down appeared to be on a half-desert island south of the equator, where a freak of geology had created a high plateau of barren rock and wind-sculpted sand, and a freak of meteorology kept the sky clear of cloud even during what their computers determined to be the counterpart of a monsoon season in these latitudes. Moreover, on the plateau, the partial pressure of oxygen was very close to Earth-normal. This was a fractionally larger planet, with a somewhat smaller and more distant moon, so at sea level its air was richer than humans were accustomed to . . . though incontestably breathable.

The landing site chosen for such admirable, commonsensical reasons had grown into the Draco Base. Cathy Polyzotis wished desperately she could be anyplace else.

Tempers were fraying and there were dismal looks on all the faces around her. Small wonder. The *Stellaris* was not a week late, not ten days late, but twelve and a half, and people were openly starting to predict that she would never come back: that there had been a war on Earth, or the Starflight Fund had been dissolved, or . . . There were nearly as many gloomy ideas circulating as there were about the fate of the Draconians.

The sky was as harsh as steel overhead. The air was full of inescapable dust borne on a breeze which never blessed this plateau with anything more refreshing than a tingle of salty mist from the waves that constantly broke on the rocky southeast coast. In the glare and heat and dryness the thirty humans on the planet fretted and argued and complained over and over about the news they were expecting from home, the indispensable new equipment they weren't going to receive and countless other disappointments.

This is making me understand the classic summary of paranoia: "The universe is a gun and they're pointing it at me!"

So many hopes had blown away on the salty wind, or evaporated towards the cruel sky. Two years ago, when she had been the youngest person ever to arrive at Sigma Draconis, she had been looking forward to the experience.

In spite of my fears about Dugal, I was excited. I . . .

She drove herself to be totally honest.

I didn't doubt my dreams. I was sure we'd solve the riddle, and convinced I would make the key contribution. And I knew Dugal was as proud of me as I was of myself. Past tense. Living two full years in the shadow of this monumental fall from greatness . . . It's not good for human beings to face the truth that a whole intelligent species can be mortal.

There was nothing superficially basic about this base; it had been designed by ingenious, thoughtful people, and though it was built of the simplest possible materials—metal plates, glass melted from local sand, and plastic processed out of a local crude oil, similar to bitumen—it was comfortable, practical, even attractive. And this, the communications and computer hall, was large enough for the thirty of them not to feel crowded together. It was not physical deprivation that was making for so many downcast looks.

How must Valentine Rorschach be feeling, who had come with the first full-manned expedition, had spent six years as the director, and was now compelled to depart with the mystery unsolved because of an arbitrary fiat from distant Earth? Was he wishing in his heart of hearts that the ship might not in fact arrive, so that he would not have to return with the knowledge of his failure?

And what about Lucas Wong, who had arrived in the second party, who notoriously did not want to inherit the directorship in addition to his departmental responsibilities as head of Biomedical Section, yet had been instructed to agree because a computer evaluation showed he was the most suitable of the senior personnel?

What about fragile, wrinkled Toko Nabura, keeping her watch at the communications console there at the far end of the hall, who had made their satellite links, and their data-storage and data-retrieval systems, into such a model of flawless reliability? How did she feel about being sent home, leaving her creation to a stranger? There was no way to judge her secret feelings, though. More than once in the past few days people had snapped at her, as though suspecting her of hiding the *Stellaris* in the crannies of hyperspace, and she had always replied in her normal soft tones, seemingly unaffected.

Yet was her fine-lipped mouth not turned down a fraction at the corners, were her eyes not a hint more narrowed than they used to be . . . ?

It looked, indeed, as though only one out of them all had kept
his cool, and that, as might have been predicted, was the chief
archeologist Igor Andrevski, a lean man in his fifties much given
to gesticulation, whose eyes were always bright under his shock of
grey hair and whose mouth seemed always to be busy with words,
or laughter, or at worst a grimace of sympathy for another person's
troubles.

He was certainly the best-liked member of the staff. In a sense
he was an atavism; he should have been born in the great days when
Schliemann at Troy, Woolley at Knossos, were converting legend
into documented fact, rather than in an age when archeology had
been distilled into a pattern of formal processes. He had been the
ideal choice to head their most important department, even though
political wrangling had delayed his appointment until 2024.

*What would we do without Igor? Thank goodness he's not due
to be rotated home! I wonder why they didn't pick him to be the
new director instead of Lucas. . . . Oh, I suppose sorting out our
occasional rows and emotional crises would drag him away too
often from what is after all the most important work we're here
to do.*

She realised with surprise that thinking about Igor had made
her smile a little. That guided her all the way to a private admis-
sion which only the strain of being isolated here (*of being afraid!*
glossed her subconscious brutally) could have provoked.

*Suppose they bring the news that Dugal has . . . died. Or even
if he hasn't! I would like, really, to have some other man in my
life. A woman should have someone else besides an invalid brother,
no matter how kind, how clever, how beloved. And out of all the
men I've met, here or at home, despite his being twice my age, I'd
like it to be Igor.*

Only somewhere a long time ago in Igor's life there had been a
tragedy. He never referred to it, but it was known that it had involved a wife he adored, and a baby, and . . .

Anyhow, they weren't there any longer, and his most profound
passions, his most forceful drives, were sublimated into that
uniquely rational form of quest for a vanished unrecoverable past:
archeology.

Perhaps if I too were to lose the person dearest to me, a bond might—

But before she had time to feel shocked at the idea welling from the depths of her mind, there was a cry from Toko.

"There she is!"

Everyone in the hall stopped in mid-word and spun to look her way. Above the communications panel, a screen where a blip had appeared, blue-white on white-green. A second elapsed, and then the hall was echoing to whoops of joy and the noise of stamping feet. The racket drowned out Toko's exchange with the ship, and it was—or felt like—a long while before anybody noticed she was not smiling in relief.

A hush fell again. Brushing back hair that was no longer there, Director Rorschach said, "Toko, is something wrong?"

"I don't know. I can't get them to talk to me. All I heard was a curt acknowledgement of contact. I think it was the young man who made his first trip last time, Somogyi. And after that, nothing. *Stellaris!* Draconis Base calling! Why are you so late this trip?"

Silence. Somebody said, "You don't suppose . . . ?" And let the words hang in the air like smoke. All of them knew about the things that could theoretically go wrong as a ship emerged from qua-space, up to and including re-entry into the normal universe as a wave of neutrinos instead of solid matter.

Toko gestured at the screen where the blip still loomed reassuringly bright, while with her other hand tapping down switch after switch on the board before her. "Nothing wrong with her automatics or power systems! There's Navigation Satellite One locking on her beam, there's Two, there's Seven just picking her up as she rounds the shoulder of the planet. . . . All normal so far as the machinery's concerned, and what's more they seem to be tracking into a first-time landing orbit—"

She was interrupted. A voice they recognised, that of Weil, boomed from the speaker rigged to receive incoming messages from the ship.

"Do not record! Wipe any automatic recording of this message! Wipe any record of the wiping! This is Rudolf Weil. We've been compelled to waste space this trip on bringing with us a military intelligence expert who's convinced you're adapting alien weaponry to conquer Earth. He's empowered to close the base and take you home if he's the slightest bit suspicious. This is my only chance to warn you, and at that I'm taking a hell of a risk. The ship is crawling with his bugs, as the base will be immediately we land. But right now he's strapped down in his cabin for the approach and our gravity compensators are oscillating, which ought to blur most of his instruments, so I've gambled on transmitting this onetime self-destruct recording. Do not on any account mention it to him, and keep your fingers crossed! *Ends!*"

IV

Going in or out of a planetary gravitation well, the compensators often wandered as they struggled to maintain a steady 1 g pull, or, to be precise in the case of a trip to Sigma Draconis, the 1.08 which they had slowly built up to in order to prepare the passengers for landing on the larger planet. Leaving Earth, the effect had been quite mild, but during the approach they had oscillated with a vengeance. By the time the creaking of the hull announced touchdown Ian was feeling very giddy.

For a while he lay in his bunk with his harness secured, listening as the faint hum of the power systems faded, and then all of a sudden found he was sniffing.

The air was growing warmer and drier, and there was an odour in it which he didn't recognise. A word burst into his mind like a magnesium flare:

Alien!

Instantly he was clawing at his harness release. Why the hell was he lying here like a dummy when outside was the whole new planet he had come here to explore?

Not pausing to pick up any of his belongings, he raced along the spinal corridor towards the main exit lock.

And stopped dead the moment he came in sight of it.

Everybody else, including the colonel, waited with impatient scowls in the lock's ante-section. The light of the new sun, reflected from a matt white bulkhead, showed that they were all staring towards the exit but making no move in that direction.

Visions of disaster filled Ian's mind. Nearest to him of the other passengers was Karen; he hurled a frantic question at her.

"The general," she explained in a soft but caustic tone, "is ensuring his immediate unpopularity. He has a bullhorn and a case full of spy-eyes. Take a look."

She moved aside. Rising on tiptoe and craning, Ian was just able to glimpse Ordoñez-Vico, framed in the lock aperture against blinding blue sky, tossing into the air literally by handfuls scores of light, off-white discs that soared away like the mythical "flying saucers" of last century.

Beyond the lock the glare was too intense for Ian to make out more than the predictable fact that the base staff had come crowding into the open, but he couldn't see their features.

Abruptly a deep voice boomed, "Who the hell are you, and what do you think you're doing?"

His first task complete, Ordoñez-Vico slammed his case shut and raised his bullhorn, which he wore on a baldric. In a crisp bark he identified himself and described his mission.

There was a stunned silence. Then there followed a roar of laughter, at first nervous, then mocking, and a clear high girl's voice shouted, "Oh, wait till you've been here a couple of days! Then you'll know the only secrets on this planet are the aliens'!"

A rattle of applause greeted the remark.

But it served mainly to make the general boil over. He raised his bullhorn again and bellowed, "You'll regret that, young woman —I promise you! Over there I see the retiring director Dr. Rorschach —come here, please. And also Dr. Toko Nabura; is that you? I propose to start my investigation immediately. Take me on a complete guided tour of this base. And I shall also require unhindered access to your computerised data stores. As for the rest of you!"

His voice rose sharply.

"You will remain here until I return, in plain sight! If one of you so much as walks around to the far side of the ship, that will be sufficient reason for me to close the base and order your immediate embarkation, bringing nothing with you, not even clothes!"

"He's out of his mind," Ian whispered.

"Have you only just realised?" Karen murmured dryly.

"Ah . . . General," said the same deep voice as before, which Ian now recognised from recordings—it sounded different uttering an angry shout from what he had heard in normal conversational tones.

"Yes, Director, what is it?"

"We may at least move into the shadow of the ship?"

"Ah . . . Very well, but remember my spy-eyes are keeping constant watch."

"And may we speak to our new colleagues?"

Ordoñez-Vico hesitated. Rorschach went on, "We're expecting news of our homes and families, you know, and of everything that's been happening on Earth. And the ship's visit *has* been somewhat delayed. . . ."

How are these people going to enjoy what they hear? The thought flashed across Ian's mind. *The Kenya-Uganda war, the Indonesian famine, the Argentine plague, that terrible tsunami with the two-thousand-mile fetch which devastated so much of South Japan, and everything else that's created such havoc recently . . . Hard to imagine all that in two short years!*

"Very well," Ordoñez-Vico said curtly. "You may talk together. But do so in plain sight of my spy-eyes at all times."

He marched pompously down the ship's external ramp and vanished from Ian's view.

"I'll be damned," Karen said, exhaling gustily. "If ever a man combined maximum gall with minimum common sense . . . Oh, well; let's get outside and see what this place really looks like."

The crew stood aside to let the passengers go out first, led by Achmed Hossein, who was due to replace Toko Nabura. Ian was last in line . . . and the moment he stepped out, the light hit him like a hammer. In his haste to leave his cabin he had omitted to bring dark glasses. But the last thing he wanted was to turn around and fetch them; even so trivial an act might make Ordoñez-Vico suspicious. He shaded his eyes with his hands, and shortly his vision adjusted enough to give him his first clear sight of mankind's precarious stellar bridgehead.

The base rested on the layer of ribbed, roughened glass into which a half-mile circle of the plateau had been fused prior to the original landing. Wind-borne sand grains had scratched and eroded it, but it was still hurtfully bright in full sunshine.

The buildings were low, and clustered together. A sort of pseudopod extended from them to and past the edge of the glass circle. That was, so to speak, the base's umbilical cord. It included a water pipe connected to a well sunk into a layer of what corresponded to chalk, where millions of litres of pure sweet rainwater had been trapped in an age when the climate hereabouts was different, and a conveyor to bring in native vegetation from the north coast, the only region where it was dense on the island. That was to supply the food converters, housed over there in a shed adjacent to the refectory and recreation complex and powered by solar mirrors on its roof. They processed the raw material into a remarkable variety of humanly edible dishes, not to mention excellent wine and beer, thanks to the care with which their master tapes had been programmed.

It had always seemed ironical to Ian that when Yakov Berendt invented the food converter he had predicted in high excitement an end to famine. How could anybody go hungry, he demanded, when every tiny village and hamlet possesses a machine capable of turning any sort of plant from trees to algae into a nourishing, even a delicious diet?

But people still starved, and not infrequently they did so by the million. Because such a machine large enough to feed even a hundred people cost as much as a light aircraft or a luxury yacht. Therefore the commonest purchasers of food converters were hotel and restaurant chains in the wealthy, not the impoverished, nations of Earth. The millennium seemed as far away as ever.

Partway along this "umbilical cord" a building stood isolated from the rest, headquarters of the civil engineering section Karen was assigned to take over. Directly below lay a vein of high-quality iron ore, and all around, of course, were vast amounts of aluminium compounds. Solar furnaces, many built right here, provided plenty of metal for building purposes and simple maintenance of the less complex equipment. Plastics were also made there, from vegetation or the tarry bitumen equivalent of which a dozen deposits were known on the mainland opposite.

Parked between there and the main portion of the base were five hovercraft: three light long-distance personnel transporters, two heavy-duty models. It was a slow way of getting around, but they floated, and by following all possible water routes, fuel requirements could be cut to a minimum, while they could cross all but the roughest ground. The base's computers had long ago worked out optimum paths to any destination on the planet, using satellite maps.

Ordinarily, apart from one on permanent reserve standby, the hovercraft would not have been here. The personnel spent most of their time far from base, digging for history.

The only people who did usually remain here were the six members of the department which Toko Nabura was now scheduled to cede to the newcomer Achmed Hossein, plus the director and hitherto the chief medical biologist, because in an emergency he must be available to save life. But that situation would now change, since the two jobs were due to be combined in the person of Lucas Wong. In any case there had been few medical emergencies; almost no local organisms could infect human tissue, and when an exception did occur, the food converters could produce a tailored antibiotic within a matter of hours—a facility which unfortunately had not become available until the third trip, or it would have saved the lives of the two people who had died here.

Likewise, there were six people in the civil engineering section, but apart from one person on base duty they were usually out at the various digs, supervising the sonic and electronic probes, the high-pressure hoses and the excavating machines needed to clear away the debris of a thousand centuries.

The biologists spent even less time here, for they were constantly studying the flora and fauna in the hope of garnering clues to the natives' disappearance, and—naturally—the archeologists were here the most seldom of all.

It looked as though they had put the last two years to good effect. All around the base were cartons and crates and cases ready for shipment to Earth. Just so, no doubt, had the artefacts Ian had studied before departure awaited their turn on the loading conveyor.

A tremor of excitement gripped him, mingled with annoyance because all that unique material was going to be flown out of his reach.

Six administrative staff, six civil engineers, eight biologists, and ten—well, I guess I should think in terms of "ten of us" now. Total, thirty. Thirty to unriddle the mysteries of an entire planet! It's absurd!

Which was as far as his musings continued before he was distracted by a cry from the girl he had heard speak up before: black-haired, green-eyed, slim, unmistakably Catherine Polyzotis. Catching sight of Weil as he emerged from the shadow of the air lock in Ian's wake, she shouted, "Rudolf! How's my brother?"

And before Weil had the chance to reply, a man's voice was exclaiming:

"I'll be damned! They actually sent Ian Macauley! Oh, that's wonderful—I never dared hope for such good luck!"

V

A moment later Ian found the celebrated Igor Andrevski pumping his hand vigorously and bombarding him with greetings, and one second later still Cathy was pushing past him to confront Weil.

"What about Dugal?" she insisted.

Memory whirred like a turbine: *Oh, yes! She's the one whose brother had—was it incurable leukemia?*

Andrevski broke off. Into a temporary local silence deep as a well Weil dropped words as heavy as stone.

"Cathy, I'm very sorry. But he was dead before we returned home."

"Oh, how tragic!" Andrevski whispered.

Ian was trying to think of something to say that would be sympathetic without being inane, when the girl simply sat down on the steps and buried her face in her hands.

Weil was about to drop beside her and put his arm around her shoulders when Andrevski checked him with a gesture.

"Leave her, Rudolf. I think I know her a little better than you do. She has been preparing herself for this bad news. Let her be alone to accept it in her own way."

Weil obeyed, although he looked doubtful, and went down to mingle with the others. Andrevski laid one thin hand on Cathy's head for a moment, and then took Ian companionably by the arm.

"Come, let me present you to the rest of your new colleagues. I can't begin to tell you how pleased I am that you are here. After seeing your amazing analysis of the inscriptions from Mohenjo-Daro, and your work on Etruscan funerary motifs, and above all your reports from Zimbabwe, I said to myself, 'That man absolutely must come to Sigma Draconis!' "

Ian suffered himself to be led along. But all the time he was mechanically shaking hands with these strangers who were not strangers, whom he had already been introduced to when they were light-years distant from him, he was thinking a single repetitive thought:

I never felt so strongly about anybody, not in my whole life, that I would sit down and weep in public at his death. I should be able to feel that deeply. I would like to. And I can't.

Overhead, like vultures, floated the spy-eyes Ordoñez-Vico had turned loose. One, no doubt drawn by some out-of-the-ordinary body secretion, swooped towards Cathy and hovered right above her.

He wondered if the lure consisted in her tears.

The wait was long and hot. After making his tour of the actual buildings, Ordoñez-Vico insisted on being shown all the alien artefacts which had so carefully been packaged for shipment, and seeing their work undone, some of the resident personnel began to grumble aloud, only to be hushed by Weil and his fellow crew members, who stressed that what the general had said was all too true; he was perfectly prepared to close the base.

"Maybe we should arrange to—ah—lose him!" someone muttered.

"Even that wouldn't help" was Weil's sour answer. "If he doesn't come back to give his personal assurance there's no plot being hatched here, that will be the end of starflight for good and all."

Still, if nothing else, this delay afforded Ian to hear the latest news of the excavations, and Andrevski was voluble on the subject. So were his other new co-workers, in particular the improbably named Olaf Mukerji whose parents had also been archeologists and who had met on a dig in the mountain fastnesses of Afghanistan, and the black American girl Sue Tennant with the short curly hair and the big disorganised teeth who had done excellent work in Mali, and Ruggiero Bono, a little tense man who despite his Italian name was Mexican by citizenship and had made notable contributions to the technique of artefact-dating, having switched to archeology from nuclear physics. And so on.

"Yes, indeed: we've located several more city-sites, and their structure and contents do indicate we were right in our guess about a single focus from which civilisation and culture diffused without interruption over the entire planet, very much unlike our own stop-and-go-and-stop pattern, hm? Maybe they didn't like to waste time! Right now we're sinking our best efforts into the one we've code-named Peat."

"Why Pete?"

"What? Oh! *P-e-a-t*, because the cover is mostly decayed vegetable matter and relatively easy to shift. I've been there a lot recently, with Cathy, who could tell you more than I can, I'm sure. Next most promising is the one we've called Ash, because it's a Pompeii situation; the cover is friable volcanic dust and also easy to shift, though unfortunately the degree of preservation is a lot poorer—there were probably earth tremors. But that's Olaf and Sue's baby, so ask them for the latest. Then there's one which we spotted on a satellite map and baptised Silt, which we're not really into yet; it's at a river mouth and seems to have been buried by fine soft mud and then heaved back towards the surface before the stuff compressed in deep water, so we're pushing ahead there as well, mostly with the hoses.

"We've been busy at the earlier sites, too, of course. Snowfall One yielded some fascinating stuff, though Snowfall Two had been subject to so much glacial action we decided we'd best leave it to a remote automatic analyser looking for anomalous concentrations of metal and such. And I'm afraid very little came of Seabed either, which we had high hopes of when the ship last called, because the aquatic life here is just as destructive as Earth's and the seawater, if anything, more corrosive, so . . ." A shrug and a wave.

Ian finally uttered the question which meant most to him: a single word.

"Inscriptions?"

"I should have mentioned them at once, shouldn't I? Yes, there have been two very important developments in that area since the ship last called. First off, Lucas's people established something that has absolutely convinced us this printed-crystal technique was their counterpart of writing. Some of the surviving species can actually imprint suitable rocks with a distorted trace of their own field—

leaving a false spoor, as it were, to mislead predators that are hunting them down. And the second thing is that at each of the sites we've opened up in the past two years, we've found what we've nicknamed libraries. Large structures, jam-packed with printed crystals, and a great many of them with good loud patterns resonating in their structure. Plus, naturally, a lot more blanked by random noise."

"How many is a great many?" Ian breathed.

"Oh, about thirty-five thousand. A few per cent."

"*What?*"

"Damn it, how many books do you find in a human library?"

"I didn't mean that. I meant . . ." Ian clenched his fists. "Have you made any progress towards deciphering them?"

Andrevski looked lugubrious. "None whatever. So far as the palaeolinguistic aspect is concerned, we're relying entirely on you. Though naturally we'll give you all the help we can."

Time had passed. A lot of time. Shadows had lengthened and the breeze was strengthening with the approach of dusk. Cathy stirred and lowered her hands from her red-rimmed eyes; instantly the dry air erased her last tears.

Poor Dugal. To have lived thirty-two years, with such a sharp mind, such splendid ambitions . . . and then to have it go for nothing. How like the natives of this world!

Stiffly she rose and walked over to the group of her colleagues who were chatting with this new arrival, this man Ian Macauley who, at least according to Igor, had done work in his twenties which deserved comparison with that of Michael Ventris and Champollion. He was gaunt and gawky, and he kept nervously plucking at his untidy red hair, but to judge by the smiles on the others' faces he was making a good impression.

As she drew near, they fell silent and looked at her. No doubt Igor would already have explained why she was sitting alone crying. Well, for the moment that was over. She felt purged of grief for the time being, able to reason and react.

"Dr. Macauley?" she said, and offered her hand. "I'm Cathy Polyzotis, as you've probably realised."

Somewhat awkwardly he shook with her, and said, "I'm—ah—I'm terribly sorry about your brother, Dr. Polyzotis."

"Cathy, please . . . Well, I was expecting it, you know. It had to happen sooner or later, and it can only happen once." She hesitated and glanced around. "Is that general going to keep us waiting here all night as well as all day?"

"He went back inside," Igor grunted. "After examining the artefacts we'd packed for dispatch. Probably wants to make sure the computer records don't describe them as ultra-guns or hyperbombs or whatever the hell."

"It makes me feel," Cathy said with a shudder, "that everybody on Earth must have gone mad."

"Not quite," Ian said. "But they're getting close."

She blinked at him, and the rest of the little group were jolted, too.

"You sound as though you mean that!" Olaf said.

"I think I do. Simply knowing that another civilisation vanished, knowing above all that the explanation may be in the records they left behind which we can't read. . . . It's preying on the mind of the human race."

"They want to be distracted at all costs," Igor suggested. "Anything so as to stop thinking about the idea."

"Yes, I'm afraid that's the size of it. The mood we left behind was . . . Well, I can only call it ugly."

Into a depressed pause there broke a booming shout from Ordoñez-Vico's bullhorn. With Toko and Rorschach following, he had emerged from the nearest building, the one housing the computers and communications gear.

"Attention, all of you! You may disperse to your quarters now. Bear in mind that my spy-eyes are monitoring literally every word and action! Assemble again in the refectory for a meal in thirty minutes. After you have eaten I propose to question you collectively, employing an advanced lie detector, and over the days to come I shall interrogate you individually, too. That is all!"

He spun on his heel and marched back indoors.

"He sounds like a prison-camp commandant!" Cathy said in horror.

Ian answered in a low tone, "Yes, he comes of the same stock. An atavism. But I'm afraid he's more typical of mankind than you or I."

VI

It would have been hard to tell, simply by looking, that this base was in fact basic. Never before in human history had so much sheer ingenuity been focussed on so tiny a spot.

When Ian reached the quarters assigned to him, pushing his belongings on a little trolley, he discovered they were amazingly spacious; he had expected far more primitive conditions—if not quite like those he was used to at archeological digs on Earth, then at any rate something cramped, like his cabin aboard *Stellaris*.

On the contrary, the bedroom was large, he had his own bathroom, there was a sonic cleanser ready to accept his soiled clothing, the walls were brightly painted and there were cheerful curtains at the window which matched the coverlet of the bed.

But, of course, they were locally spun from the same material used for flooring, and packaging delicate alien artefacts, and the table and the two chairs—one upright, one easy—were made of the same stuff, and the floor and the walls and the door and the ceiling and the bathtub and the shelves were all variants of the same simple metal plate with a foamed internal layer which was the best the foundry and machine shop here could offer, anodised with several colours.

The changes were, nonetheless, very ingeniously rung. He was impressed—as impressed as he had been when, thinking in despair that his mass allotment of twenty kilos would mean leaving behind half the reference books and computer programmes he wanted to bring with him, he had discovered just how many data could be crammed into a single cassette of acceleratape when expense was virtually no object.

He had wound up scratching his head and trying to decide what else he ought to take along.

And he was positively shaken when he saw the variety of food offered in the cafeteria-styled refectory, which included every classic dish from every cuisine on Earth, plus a choice of more than fifty drinks to wash it down.

And to think my briefing covered that in a single sentence— something like, "The machines provide a diet both nutritionally adequate and exceptionally varied."

He was frankly goggling at the array of selection knobs when Karen Vlady tapped his arm and murmured, "Ian dear, in the next two years you'll have a chance to try them all!"

A valid point, in the light of which it didn't seem to matter that this first time he wound up, somehow, with bird's-nest soup, *souvlakia,* mealie porridge with okra sauce, and peaches Melba. It all tasted most convincing.

The refectory doubled as a lounge and conference hall. Around its walls were plastic couches, foamed, formed and furred in a single operation, light enough to be carried by one person if it was desired to rearrange the room. In the centre of the floor were stack-able chairs and a dozen tables, each capable of seating four people.

Ordoñez-Vico had arrived early and created for himself a sort of place of honour, with Rorschach, Wong and Weil as his companions. He ate little, but kept sweeping the room with a defiant, challeng-ing glare.

Ian accepted an invitation to sit with Cathy and Andrevski, with Olaf, Sue, Ruggiero and Irene Bakongu—who seemed to be an old and close friend of Ruggiero's—at the next table. Even though An-drevski kept urging him to take another and yet another glass of a delicious white wine, based on a tape delivered by the second ex-pedition which had retained extraordinarily fine detail despite countless replayings, Ian found the meal a terrible ordeal. Ordoñez-Vico's spy-eyes had found their way indoors, inevitably, and one of them clung to the ceiling directly above their table like a patch of mould.

Moreover the knowledge weighed on him: *This is all of us, and very nearly all we have!*

Comparing this base to the planet as a whole was like comparing one human life-span to the period since the disappearance of the natives.

He was not alone in lacking appetite. Much food was left on many plates . . . not that it mattered, for it would all be recycled through the processors. When the tension had reached near breaking point, Ordoñez-Vico finally rose, cleared his throat and produced his lie detector.

"Your attention, please! First I propose to make some calibrations. I shall put some questions, and pick on one of you at random to supply the answer."

He left his seat and followed a weaving path through the hall which took him past every table. His glance darted from face to face, then to his lie detector, then back again. It was noticeable that his eyes paused a fraction longer when he looked at the women, as though he resented their presence.

And it was a woman he called on to answer his first question: Toko Nabura.

"These aliens—how long ago did they die out?"

"About a hundred thousand years, plus or minus four thousand."

"Why aren't you more precise about the date? You!" And a woman again: Sue Tennant.

Wearily she replied, "This is a world with vigorous tectonics and rapid changes of climate. It's hard to calibrate the strata."

"Yet you assert that their earliest traces are only some three thousand years prior to their last. How do you explain that?" He was pointing at a woman again, and this time at Cathy.

She had spent the meal in a brown study of depression, eating little, speaking only when addressed. Now, though, she contrived to rouse herself and find an answer.

"Oh . . . Oh, everything points to it."

"I want details!" Ordoñez-Vico strode over to her. "Don't think you can get away with vague double-talk!"

"General!"—sharply, from Andrevski. "Cathy was told, only a few hours ago, that her brother died after she left Earth."

"I know all about that, and I still want a proper answer!"

All around the hall chairs scraped as people pushed them back resignedly. This was going to be long and unpleasant, that was plain.

But by now Cathy had all her wits about her and was looking Ordoñez-Vico straight in the eye. She said, "With respect, General, I'm not sure you'd understand if I said that the phi-diffusion factor in the modified orthorhodoclosites, the pyruvitic gangliar formations, and the Type G-9 artefacts which are the main items in respect of which we've so far established a definite temporal progression—because they are found at all the sites we've investigated rather than at one or two—when taken in conjunction with contemporary C-14 uptake in surviving near relatives of the natives, and the known decay rate of epidermal pseudo-chitin as established by testing it in various simulable media that correspond to actual conditions at the various city-sites . . . and sundry other factors, naturally . . . all these things are what we base our estimates upon, and they happen to coincide within a very narrow band of the past: three thousand years. But equally I *am* sure"—this with a sunny smile—"that you as an expert in your field will take an expert's word in a field you're not conversant with. Won't you?"

From the far side of the hall there was a noise as though somebody was trying to stifle a laugh, without much success. Ordoñez-Vico whirled, as though suspecting mockery, but all he saw was Achmed Hossein holding a napkin to his mouth and a great many polite smiles at surrounding tables.

As for Ian, he wanted to clap his hands. But all he dared do was give Cathy a wink, which she acknowledged with a moue before reaching for the wine bottle.

Breathing heavily, Ordoñez-Vico rounded on Rorschach.

"You've been here six years—why haven't you come up with any solid facts?"

Rorschach, as usual, brushed at his bald forehead as though

still expecting to find on it the hair he had lost since his arrival.

"But we have. A great many. As a result of slow, thorough research, particularly by comparing the scanty remains of the intelligent species themselves—I mean their fragmentary corpses—with their nearest surviving relatives. Of which there are about four hundred and fifty, aren't there, Lucas? I'm talking about species, obviously."

"Nearly five hundred when you take genetic resemblances into account," Lucas Wong said with a sigh.

"So what are these solid facts?" Ordoñez-Vico barked. "I didn't notice them when I was going through your reports on Earth!"

Rorschach allowed that point to sink into the minds of everybody else present by hesitating just sufficiently long before he answered.

"This is almost cruel!" Cathy breathed.

"He deserves it," Ian muttered.

"Well, for example," Rorschach said, looking up at the ceiling, "we know they were very much like us in some respects. We know they were interested in the universe around them. We suspect they traded among each other. We're almost certain they had the equivalent of writing, and beyond doubt they had transportation, communication, science, mathematics. . . . But we also know that in some ways they were very different from mankind. Above all, their culture must have been as influenced as all human cultures have always been by sex."

He paused, having judged—rightly, as was clear—that he had used a word which in the general's vocabulary was of limited significance, and pejorative into the bargain.

"What do you mean?"

"I think you'd better ask Lucas, rather than me," Rorschach suggested.

"I will decide who is to answer which question. In this case . . . you!"

He pointed at Nadine Shah, a handsome woman (a woman again, as though he really believed he could catch one in a lie more easily than he could a man) in her late forties, who was Lucas's chief assistant and the leading authority present on comparative biology.

In a clear voice she replied, "Unless they were improbably different from their surviving cousins, they were bisexual as we are, but both sexes coexisted in the same individual. Infancy was a neuter stage; there followed a male stage; and after that there was a comparatively short female stage prior to the infertility of old age."

That, for the moment, silenced Ordoñez-Vico, and gave Rudolf Weil the chance to say, "That's new, isn't it?"

Nadine nodded. "Yes, when you last called we were still under the misapprehension that we were dealing with no more than an extreme degree of sexual differentiation. Now we've actually tracked several individuals through the transition stage. It lasts about a year, after which what was a functional male is incontestably a functional female. There are terrestrial parallels, of course, such as oysters."

"Kindly do not talk among yourselves!" Ordoñez-Vico snapped. "Simply answer my questions!"

Obediently the company fell silent again.

"Explain more about the differences between them and us. You!" Pointing now at Ruggiero Bono.

"They thought differently from the way we do, and that's the long and short of it," sighed the little dark man. "They approached problems similar to ours by a different route. Up there on the moon they equipped their telescope with—with something organic, where we'd have used solid-state electronics. We dug that flying machine out from under a pile of snow, and from that and everything else that's reasonably intact we've deduced that they could store enormous amounts of energy in ways we'd regard as fit only for a kid's toy: like twisting rubber bands! They used springs and filaments, except somehow they managed to pack the energy right away on the molecular level. Oh, they did things we can barely guess at!"

"So what happened to them?" Ordoñez-Vico rapped, and pointed at Andrevski for the answer.

Perfectly calm and collected, the chief archeologist wiped a trace of wine from his upper lip and planted both elbows on the table with a thoughtful expression. "Well, a great many possibilities remain open," he said judiciously. "I'll list them with their various

pros and cons, keeping track as best I can. There's the possibility
that they may have emigrated, to begin with."

"What?"

"Well, as I said, many possibilities remain open! Myself, I don't
think that's to be seriously considered. More to the point, perhaps,
is the idea of epidemic disease. We know they had rapid transportation, so it's conceivable that they may have spread some fatal virus
so swiftly around the planet they had no chance to develop immunity against it. On the other hand, the bioelectronics on the
moon, which have just been mentioned, argue that they must have
been very skilled in organic chemistry. It's reasonable to assume that
their medicine too would have been very advanced.

"Did they exterminate themselves in a war? Well, we've found
no traces to suggest that any of their cities were laid waste by other
than the natural forces: weathering, earthquakes and suchlike.
But it's not impossible, even though we've ruled out explosives,
nuclear or otherwise, and massive doses of any substance we know
to be poisonous to the contemporary fauna. And radiation weapons,
too. It's been suggested that some disease may have been deliberately
sown broadcast—in other words, they may have fought a biological
war—but there's an excellent reason for discarding that idea, too."

"What?"

"How could they have crammed such a vast range of achievement into so short a time if they'd wasted any of their ingenuity
on quarrelling among themselves? We've surveyed this planet from
space over and over and over; we've probed the surface with sonar,
electronic detectors, all our most reliable techniques. We've found a
coherent cross section of relics. In three thousand years they went
from—oh—what we'd call the Neolithic stage, smelting copper and
baking pottery vessels, to spaceflight. It took us more than twice as
long."

"How do you know these conditions didn't exist simultaneously?"
Ordoñez-Vico broke in. "They do on Earth!"

"A very acute question," Andrevski acknowledged. "Let me make
my point a little clearer. We have found a central focus from which
their culture appears to have disseminated—the sole place at which
the full range of artefacts has been discovered. As one progresses

along a line of expansion, or more exactly a cone of expansion, because it broadens as it grows longer, the lower level disappears. At
the far side of the planet from this focus I mentioned, there seem
to be *no* primitive vessels, *no* copper implements, *no* artefacts that
can be dated to the earlier, rather than the later, stage of their development. It's as though, to take an earthly analogy, the civilisation
which arose in the Fertile Crescent had expanded without interruption westwards, engulfed Europe, crossed to North America, then
spread to the far side of the Pacific, expanded over the whole of
Asia and India and returned to its still-intact point of origin,
where, naturally, things would by then have been very much
changed. This is another thing to bear in mind when considering
the possibility of them being wiped out in a war: this single continuous expansion, as though they never met any opposition. Without opposition, what cause for war? But—" Andrevski raised an
admonitory finger. "This brings in a related subject, one which I
presume to have been at the forefront of the minds of those who
sent you. Were they wiped out by an attack from space?"

Someone gave vent to a nervous titter. Ordoñez-Vico quelled it
with a glare like a flamethrower.

"Go on!"

Andrevski studied his hands with intent concentration.

"This hypothesis assumes the existence of yet another species, so
jealous of its privileges that it scours the galaxy in search of possible
competitors, and upon discovering them attacks without mercy. Am
I correct in guessing that this is what's worrying people at home?"

Ordoñez-Vico hesitated; then he said with an air of defiance, "Yes!"

"I see. As a matter of fact, I carried out quite an exhaustive computer analysis of this idea when it first occurred to me. It led to a
pair of extremely interesting conclusions: on the one hand, any
such species with the technology to attain space travel would stand
between an eighty-nine and a ninety-nine per cent chance of fighting a disastrous final war before reaching another star, and on the
other, assuming it did discover hyperflight, it would have technology adequate to sterilise whole planets, not simply to hunt down
members of one particular race. In sum, General, if that were why
the natives disappeared, the odds are several thousand to one in

favour of this planet having become a belt of asteroids . . . which I think you'll concede it has not?"

Moment by moment Ordoñez-Vico's cheeks were growing redder, as though he suspected he was being mocked but could not put his finger on precisely how.

"Then what other explanations can you offer?" he snapped.

"Oh, several!" Andrevski said, and in parenthesis to Cathy: "More wine, please; this is making me thirsty. . . . Yes, several, as I was saying. I believe we can rule out predators straightaway, because there are no large predators on the planet at present, and without being kept in check by the intelligent race one would expect them to have multiplied if they existed. That is, unless their diet consisted exclusively of their intelligent cousins, and having eaten the last of their prey they starved to death—not, I submit, particularly likely, hm? Parasites, of course, are another matter; it's been correctly remarked that human body lice would not survive mankind, but again none of the surviving species is disastrously infected with parasites capable of killing them wholesale.

"Did their religion call for them to sacrifice one another, and ultimately reach such a pitch of fanaticism that groups and factions competed to see who could slay the most hecatombs on the most frequent feast days? It's not without its earthly parallels, that notion. One might cite the downfall of the Inca culture, the wars of religious intolerance, the Inquisition, the *autos-da-fé* where dissenters were publicly burned alive. . . . Oh, I'm sorry. I should have asked whether you're religious."

"Yes!"

"I am not, myself, but I don't wish to give offence. Let me leave that aside, then—because in any event it's most unlikely. All our evidence points to a planned, rational, successful expansion from a single centre, as I explained, so that kind of lunatic brutality would only enter the picture if we strained our definition of religion to include an ideology like Nazism . . . the most colourable of this particular range of suggestions in my view, by the way. A single-minded dictator, perhaps born of an exceptionally intelligent species—that could be the explanation we're looking for."

"Appearing out of nowhere?"

"Ah, that's what's most ingenious about this favourite hypothesis of mine," Andrevski said, beaming. "Let's suppose that two events fell very close in the history of this world: first, some solar disturbance irradiated the planet and provoked a higher-than-normal incidence of mutation, including one which generated intelligence. Remarkable intelligence! Constant expansion followed for three thousand years, until the small original nucleus of intelligent creatures had explored the whole planet—or rather, their descendants had—and visited the moon. And *then* came a fatal setback: the planet's magnetic field underwent a periodic reversal, like those we know about on Earth. They perceived their surroundings in terms of electromagnetic fields, they most likely communicated in the same mode, their entire world picture was dependent on such effects. Suddenly . . . they went insane. Because they had all, simultaneously, lost touch with reality. How does that appeal to you, General?"

Andrevski sat back with a smug expression, while Ordoñez-Vico was visibly floundering in the welter of his words.

"A great theory," Rudolf Weil said dryly. "Except that it doesn't hang together. There wasn't any such solar flare-up; it would have left traces on the rocks of the moon, and we eliminated that idea on the first trip."

"And the last two magnetic-field reversals here were forty thousand years too early and thirty-eight thousand years too late respectively," Ruggiero added. "Oh, Igor!"

Not a whit abashed, Andrevski said, "I know, I know! But it would be such an elegant explanation if it were true, wouldn't it?"

It was beginning to dawn on the general that he had been led a very long way up a very twisted garden path. One instant before he erupted Rorschach said hastily, "What it comes to really, General, is that we've been driven back on the supposition that the natives' downfall was due to some flaw in their constitution, but that it must have been one which affected them differently from us. Maybe their sudden rise to planetary domination was due to a—well, a form of drug. Perhaps some local food plant mutated into a form which stimulated their intelligence, but had long-term effects on their metabolism or their breeding capacity. Or perhaps it was killed off by a blight. I grant you that's improbable for the same reason that an epidemic is improbable, but we're groping around in the dark, we really are!"

During this speech the general had been recovering his self-control by consulting his lie detector and taking a great many deep and rapid breaths.

He said now, "My impression is that you do not believe I mean what I say. Well, I do not believe you, either! This device of mine"—he held it up—"has not revealed any direct falsehoods . . . but Dr. Andrevski has attempted to confuse me with what he promptly confessed to be an indirect falsehood! By that I mean a web of words designed to lead his listeners astray. Be warned! It is not my responsibility to prove that you are lying. It is your responsibility to prove beyond any shadow of doubt that you are telling the truth, the whole truth and nothing but the truth! Starting tomorrow, early, I shall interrogate each of you in turn, in depth and in detail. And if anybody tries to deceive me, you know what will happen. Now, if somebody will guide me back to my quarters . . . ?"

When the general had gone, Cathy said, her face very pale, "A man like that was chosen by the U.N. to be their representative, to sift through our data and pester us with questions. . . . No, I simply don't believe it!"

"I suspect Ian could tell you how horribly true it is," Andrevski muttered.

"Yes indeed," Ian said. "But don't forget—his spy-eyes are monitoring everything we say, and he may conceivably have the patience to play through every tape from every last one of them. I think we'd better go quietly and quickly to our beds."

VII

Thanks to Ordoñez-Vico, the normal work of the ship's thirty-day stopover was going ahead far more slowly than usual; still, it was going ahead after a fashion. Ten days after the landing Weil was busy supervising the loading of the first Earth-bound packages into the hold made empty by delivery of the new equipment which was now being distributed to the various departments, chiefly more refined remote-analysis gear. There had been a major breakthrough in that field—ironically, as a by-product of counter-terrorist measures. Most of the new devices had first been used to spot mail bombs and concealed weapons at frontier posts and airports.

Thanks to the general's meddling, most of the packages had had to be remade after he opened them for inspec :on.

"Morning, Rudolf," a voice said from behind I m, and he turned to find Rorschach approaching.

"Morning, Valentine," Weil answered. "How are things going?"

"Oh . . . not too badly, considering. Everybody has behaved extremely well. By this time I wouldn't have been surprised if someone had punched Ordoñez-Vico in the jaw."

"Nor would I," Weil agreed. "I've sometimes been tempted . . ." He mopped his face, sighing. "When I think of all the things I wanted to see on this visit, I get furious. This isn't in the least how I expected to use up my last few days here. And I bet it isn't how you expected to use yours."

Rorschach hesitated. "Well—ah . . . They aren't going to be my last few days, after all."

"What?"

"The fact that you have to take Ordoñez-Vico back with you means only nine personnel can be rotated. So I'll drop off the list. Lucas never wanted to become director, you know, and I don't think he deserves to have the job forced on him. My health is good, I have no special ties on Earth and I think I'm reasonably well liked by the staff. So I'll stay."

Weil gave a whistle. "What does the general think about that idea?"

"He doesn't know yet. But I have plenty of good reasons to offer him—not that one can be sure he's susceptible to reason, hm? Ah . . . There's one thing that's been troubling me, you know."

"Only one?" Weil uttered a sour chuckle. "That being . . . ?"

"Is there a real risk of us being stranded? I mean, even if we persuade the general those rumours about alien weapons are groundless, is there a chance that the fund may be abolished anyway?"

"Yes, I'm afraid there is."

"I thought you'd say that." Eyes concealed behind dark glasses because the glare out here was as ever fierce, Rorschach looked towards the western horizon. "Would they give us at least some kind of link with home? Perhaps a cheap automatic qua-space missile that would shuttle back and forth carrying news and data?"

"The suggestion has been made, but it was turned down."

"What?"

"It was blocked by the same sort of paranoid suspicion that sent Ordoñez-Vico here. A joint Russo-American-Japanese consortium published plans for just such a robot ship, quite cheap, very reliable, capable of being put into service in little more than a year. Do I have to explain what became of the proposal?"

Rorschach said bitterly, "Another plot by the rich to keep secrets from the poor. The builders would have first crack at our alien science."

"Cynical! But all too accurate. Nonetheless, you can rest assured that when I get home I'm going to devote the remainder of my active life to fighting that sort of shortsighted idiocy. If I have anything to do with it, the base here won't be cut off. After all, the data we're taking back include a good many exciting new discoveries, and perhaps . . . No, it's probably too much to hope for."

"So I gather from talking to our new recruits," Rorschach sighed, turning to look at the base buildings again. "They all paint a very dismal picture. Crisis on crisis, famine, epidemics, all these petty wars about nothing much, and here and there signs of a major war. Correct?"

"Yes."

"I sometimes wonder, you know, whether there's an inevitable limit to the achievements of intelligent beings. The natives here—now mankind, not for the first time on the brink of suicide . . . It reminds me of the old joke question: Is there intelligent life on Earth? And we're the first people in a position to wonder about it seriously."

With all too obvious an air of changing the subject, Weil said, "Speaking of the new recruits, how do they impress you?"

"Oh, I think we'll get on well together. I'm sure Achmed will handle the communications and computer side most competently, and Karen Vlady is extremely likable as well as being admirably qualified, and—oh, the lot of them strike me as ideal for our kind of existence. Bar one, to be candid, and I'd like your opinion about him."

"Not by any chance Ian Macauley?"

"That's right."

"Yes, he's something of an oddity, isn't he? Tense and remote, and seeming to live somewhere different from the rest of us. But Igor was delighted to get him, wasn't he?"

"Oh yes, and at present he appears to be settling in well and making a good impression on his colleagues. I can't say why it is I'm concerned about him; I just know I am. What do you think?"

"I'd back him to crack the native language."

"You honestly believe he's that good?"

"He has a great deal of determination. I could tell, the moment I met him, he'd had to fight a hell of a battle against himself before agreeing to be sent here. He hated the prospect of being shut up with a dozen near strangers in the ship, but he overcame that, too, and made himself popular during the voyage. Yes, I think he has it in him to batter away until he makes a breakthrough. But he'll probably go about it some very personal and unexpected way."

Rorschach glanced at his watch. "I hope," he muttered, "that he doesn't do anything personal and unexpected today. The general is spending the morning in the relic shed with him, Cathy and Igor, being told about the printed crystals they brought in from the peat site. It's the most explosive situation yet. Ian's unpredictable, as you just said; Igor made it clear the first evening that he thinks the general is a blockhead, and Cathy . . . well, she seems to have recovered well from the shock of hearing about her brother, but she's a deep person and hides her feelings much too often."

He brightened slightly. "Well, at any rate if we get through today intact, things should be easier from tomorrow on. The next thing Ordoñez-Vico wants is a sight of our working methods, so he's going to let us get back on the job. Having something to do will bleed off a lot of our accumulated tension."

I wish that bloody man would get off our necks! I want to start work on these printed crystals he doesn't give a hoot for. Back on Earth I had how many through my hands—eighteen, nineteen? And most of their patterns scrambled. But here there are hundreds, and at the digs there are thousands, and I'm itching, absolutely itching to get at them!

Restless, Ian paced up and down the aisles between the bare metal storage racks of the relic shed—not the original, which had been made of steel plates, but a hastily erected substitute of plastic and aluminium, with minimal magnetic sensitivity.

All around him were thousands of relics brought in from various digs, those in the best state of preservation or found in what appeared to be significant conjunction with one another. But every last one was horribly enigmatic. A sort of pear-shaped thing here, with a hook on the narrow end, about a metre and a half long . . . and next a cluster of five corroded bars, like the frame of a child's swing . . . and next a sort of plate, a concave shallow disc with four large and four small protuberances spaced equidistantly around its circumference . . . and there other and always other artefacts, purpose unknown and unguessed.

But I've got to make guesses and start making them right away!

He glanced around. There was some kind of low-key argument

going on at the far end of the shed, where in an open space a big bench held an array of scientific equipment—radio daters, neutron-bombardment analysers, various chemical analysers, and a computer remote with a metre-wide screen and the controls which linked it to the base's main computers. It sounded as though it might continue for some while.

Almost guiltily he picked up the five corroded bars and examined them. They were large and heavy, and one of them was half a metre shorter than the rest.

Now, if I were a crab-shaped six-limbed creature with electro-magnetic perceptions, what the hell would I use that for? I—hmm! Interesting! I think it was meant to stand upright, and if it were just a little more spread out . . . Where's that disc? How big is it?

He leaned the clustered bars against a strut and picked the disc up. It also was very heavy, but if it were laid on the ground . . . and if that hook-tipped what's-it were . . .

Hmm! He rubbed his chin, staring at the items arranged side by side. *Now, if only—*

"Cathy!" he shouted. "This group here, coded Ash 5248 through 5250! Were any organic remains found in association with the metal bits?"

The altercation at the far end of the shed broke off.

"Macauley!" Ordoñez-Vico snapped. "Don't interrupt when I'm talking to—here, what do you think you're doing?"

He came storming down the aisle with Igor and Cathy anxiously following.

Ian licked his lips in embarrassment. "I'm sorry. I just had an idea about how these might fit together, and even what they might be for. But it's probably ridiculous."

"Really!" The general's voice dropped to a purr. "Now, I've just been told in great detail that nobody knows whether these things do anything or not, let alone what the natives used them for. I'm delighted to hear you contradict that. Continue!"

Cathy and Igor were both looking furious, and Ian felt the blood rush to his cheeks. He muttered, "Well—ah . . . If these things are numbered consecutively, I presume they were found together?"

Cathy gave a sour nod.

"Were they by any chance in some kind of large enclosed space, what you might call a hall?"

Cathy started, and her annoyance faded like frost at sunrise. "Yes, they were! I recall how excited Olaf was when he got into that building. And he found a great many other similar groups of metal bars, but this is the only one he shipped back to base. It seemed typical, he said."

"Why did you ask about organic remains in association?" Igor demanded, likewise forgetful of his anger.

"Well—uh . . ." Ian picked up the pear-shaped object in two fingers. "This is very light, isn't it? But that disc and these bars are very heavy and solid. Suppose the bars were set up over the disc"— he made illustrative gestures with down-turned fingers—"and this bob were hung from the crosspiece so it could swing freely. You'd need to prevent it being blown around by draughts, wouldn't you? So you'd close the lot in with something nonmetallic, like cloth or matting, and there you'd have it."

"Have what?" Igor barked.

"Uh . . . Well, wouldn't a species with electromagnetic senses be very interested in the approach of an electrical storm? Particularly if they were in some kind of shelter, and wanted to decide whether to leave it or not on a longish journey."

There was a dead pause. Then, all of a sudden, Cathy said, "Barometer!"

"What?" Ian blinked at her.

"Something I found at the peat site and couldn't make head or tail of: a sort of bellows arrangement, but collapsed." She slapped herself on the forehead. "Why in hell haven't I programmed the computers with data about storm-warning devices? Ian, this is incredible! It makes dozens of things fit which never occurred to me before!"

Igor let go a great gust of laughter and flung his arms around Ian in an exuberant embrace.

"Very interesting!" Ordoñez-Vico said in an acid voice. "A complete stranger arrives here for the first time, and in a matter of days he makes sense of something which I've been assured made *no* sense. I find that a most suspicious circumstance. Why, pray, have you pleaded such total ignorance?"

There was another pause, but this time it crackled. It stretched to five seconds, ten—and then Ian clenched his fists, his face as red as fire, and took a pace to confront Ordoñez-Vico.

"Because, damn it, there are a mere thirty people looking at a whole damn' planet across a hundred thousand years! You don't seem to understand what's involved! Listen! You come from La Paz, don't you? Right: imagine it without its people. It stands there empty. No one clears that blocked drain. The rains cause a flood. Dead leaves build up in the gutters, they rot and seeds start to sprout, blown from gardens and parks. Weeds blot out the flowers. The paving stones twist and heave as the tree roots burrow under them; grass grows in the cracks, moss and lichens appear on the walls as the foundations of the buildings shift. The glass cracks in the windows, and the rain blows in, and the wooden furniture starts to rot and crumble. Books dissolve into a soggy mess, birds flit in and make nests on the shelves and insects take shelter in closets and bathrooms and behind oil paintings. Fungi move in, too, and creepers, and mould. Wind-borne dust gathers in corners both outside and inside the buildings; soon, that's also overgrown."

His eyes were focussing somewhere far beyond the face of the astonished general, at whom he appeared to be staring.

"There's a landslip somewhere. A concrete wall collapses, opens a whole building to the weather. There's a temblor, and a hundred buildings fall. All that can happen in one hundred years, and it's only the beginning. La Paz after a century, tumbledown, covered with creepers, the home of wild animals and snakes and butterflies and birds—how much could you tell about the way of life of a human family by burrowing into the rubble and rotting leaf mould, hm—if you were from another planet and had never seen a live human being? Ask yourself that! Here's a piano frame—but you have no ears, you never imagined music! Here's a tableknife—but you don't eat, you only drink liquids! Here's a sewing machine—but you have fur and don't wear clothes! After one century, how much sense would you make of what remained? And we're not talking about a hundred years here. We're talking about a hundred thousand! Ignorance? Don't make me laugh! It's taken genius for the people here to find out what they do know, and it's small thanks to the shortsighted fools who picked on you to come and pester them!"

He spun on his heel and marched away.

For a long, long moment Cathy and Igor stood with their eyes shut, expecting the landslide to crash down. But the general remained curiously silent. They blinked at him. He was very pale and seemed at a loss.

"Ah . . ." he forced out at length. "I believe—yes, for the time being I've seen enough of what's in here. You may carry on with your work. Good morning!"

And he, too, turned away, with slow worried steps, towards the exit and the bright subtropical sunshine.

VIII

Now for the verdict . . . !

The staff, both those scheduled to remain and those about to depart, were visibly nervous as they congregated at the refectory to hear the result of Ordoñez-Vico's investigation. The most nervous of them all—and the last to arrive, apart from Rorschach, who was accompanying the general—was Ian.

He hesitated a long time outside the door, his head in a whirl.

I never thought so short a time could pack so many impressions into my memory!

They all seemed to swarm up to consciousness at once.

Seen from the hovercraft in which they had crossed to the mainland of the nearer continent: a flock of bright globular flying creatures rising to greet the dawn, more like jellyfish than any earthly bird—supported by ballonets of hydrogen, expanding as the day grew warmer and allowing them to float inland off the breeze from the ocean, there to trap blown seeds and tiny insectlike creatures on sticky tentacles by way of food until evening came and the wind again carried them back towards the shore and the tops of the trees where they passed the night.

Trees? Not exactly. But tall plants with drooping tendrils and many close-set pale green plaques on each that absorbed sunlight and at night shrank close to the stems again to conserve heat.

On a grasslike sward that stretched nearly to the horizon: a herd of animals related to the vanished natives, draped in loose dark blue or dark red skin almost as thick and tough as that of a rhinoceros,

...ythmically—their upper and lower carapaces pumping ...down like a bellows and an orifice at each end of the body ...pening and shutting in turn—while they cropped the underbrush.

And, stalking them, a small predator with four incredibly long walking legs and its frontal appendages reduced to a counterpart of fangs: two deadly-sharp horny daggers.

And on the rocky floor of an old volcanic caldera: a colony of brownish creatures from the same general category complete with their female elders; these latter, huge and sedentary and swollen with their embryonic young, basking in sunlight while young active males brought them succulent branches, funguslike growths and —why, nobody yet knew—chunks of rock as big as a man's head.

And at the first site he was taken to: humming machines quartering back and forth on the floor of a pit already some fifteen metres deep, automatically determining with gentle sonic probes whether anything solid lay under the cover of decayed vegetation, then yielding place to the other machines which cut the cover away with high-pressure water jets and gathered it up and brought it to a conveyor that took it over the crest of the next low hill and piled it into a huge spoil heap.

There he had seen alien artefacts uncovered, not by the score or the hundred, but by the thousand in the course of one single day: every precious scrap being sifted out, labelled, photographed, probed and reported to the computers back at base by way of a line-of-sight relay on the hilltop. Other, more distant sites had to report by satellite, but this was the closest.

All the appurtenances of what humans would call a city were here: buildings, most collapsed but some still roofed, and streets and roadways; what might be warehouses or shops; what might be a laboratory; what might be some kind of temple, perhaps, or public meeting place, in a complex at the centre with a library—a store of printed crystals—and hivelike dwellings equipped with water pipes, air vents, mysterious charcoal-like bars sunk in the walls; what might have been a market, or possibly a botanical park, for before the site was buried species of plant from the other continent had managed to seed and grow through a few seasons. . . .

And there were vehicles, or their skeletons, with a wheel at the front and two behind and the space between full of some substance that had rotted very quickly and left only a few stripes of metal to indicate its actual shape, and there were articles made of glass, and many of metal, and what must certainly have been trays and dishes and containers, and what correspondingly could never have been anything used by creatures shaped like men.

Puzzling niches marked the walls facing the streets. More were to be found indoors, but these people had never fitted doors, just doorways. There were traces of organic compounds in all niches, but those outside were different from those within.

So much—so incredibly much!

Despair darkened Ian's mind.

To think that my fit of bad temper may have put paid to all the effort that's been sunk in the project! Oh, they haven't said as much, nobody has even mentioned the idea, but—I'm a fool!

He drew a deep breath, summoned his courage and finally joined the rest of the staff in the refectory. They glanced at him, and a few nodded, but they were all waiting for Ordoñez-Vico.

In silence Ian sat down, by himself, near the door, and waited likewise.

All the while he was touring the digs, the general had been quiet and sullen. He had listened a great deal, and constantly consulted his lie detector, but said hardly anything. Three days ago he had returned and called in his spy-eyes, and settled to the chore of analysing their records. Since then, gloom had gathered until it was like a fog shutting out the sunlight; one wanted to shiver even at high noon.

One or two people had said flatly that even if they were ordered to, they were not going to go home. They did not sound as though they expected to be believed.

Small wonder. To be marooned with a group of thirty would be bad; with a third as many, or a fifth . . .

And here was Ordoñez-Vico in his sprucest uniform, and Rorschach bending like any restaurant waiter to pull and push his chair as he sat down. It was impossible to read any emotion on the director's face.

The general looked around the room slowly, his eyes picking out Ian and lingering on him; Ian quailed inwardly.

And then he spoke.

"It is time for me to state what report I propose to make to the U.N. Shorn of its details, it runs like this. The scientists here are contending with a nearly insuperable task, but they have made astonishing progress under great difficulties and deserve the maximum possible continuing support."

There was a moment of stunned silence. Then there was an almost hysterical outburst of laughter, cheers and clapping. Ian sat bewildered, staring at the still pale face of the general.

Who waited until the tumult died away, and then went on: "It is, I believe, fair for me to say that my mission was not wholly the fault of those on Earth. To some extent you have yourselves to blame that the true difficulties you are facing are not correctly appreciated at a distance of nineteen light-years. One is accustomed to imagine that modern science is capable of practically anything; have we not, after all, broken through what was for long held to be the ultimate natural barrier, the speed of light? For my own part, until Dr. Macauley painted so clear a picture for me that I could almost see it in front of my eyes, I was not—to use a crude but appropriate phrase —'feeling it in my guts.' I'm obliged to Dr. Macauley, and so should you be."

Everybody turned to look at Ian, and there was another burst of clapping. Ian remained as still as a statue.

"I have just two more things to say. First, Director Rorschach has volunteered to remain for another tour, owing to the fact that I must return and will take up space and food and air in the *Stellaris*. I am impressed with his record of achievement and will support his decision when I get home.

"And, second"—he licked his lips—"I believe I may have offended several of you. I apologise. I had braced myself for what I knew would be a distasteful task. I had not expected to find it was also absurd. I wish you all the best of luck."

And this time the clapping was for him, while he sat stiff and immobile with tiny beads of perspiration pearling down his forehead.

Then the meeting broke up and everybody rushed at Ian—who
fled for the exit and the corridor leading to the seclusion of his
room, leaving his colleagues behind to stare at one another in astonishment.

This was Ian's door. Cathy tapped at it. Beyond, there was a
sound of movement and then a weary question: "Who is it?"

"Cathy. May I come in?"

Faintly, music could be heard. There was a celebratory party in
progress in the refectory. Traditionally there was a party just before
the ship's departure, but this was for a better reason than ever
before.

"Ah . . . Just a second." The lock clicked, and there he was,
rather shyly gazing at her.

"May I come in?"

"Well—of course." And as she stepped over the threshold, he went
on, "I'm sorry I disappeared; it was very rude of me. But I'd been so
sure I'd sabotaged the whole project, and when it turned out I'd
done the opposite, I simply couldn't believe it. . . . Well, what can
I do for you?"

She looked at him levelly for a long moment. Then she said,
"I suddenly realised that I want to kiss you."

"What?"

"You heard me."

"Yes, but . . ." He shook his head blankly. "Why?"

"*Why?*" She almost stamped her foot. "How can a man be so
brilliant *and* so obtuse? Listen, Ian. What agonies you've been
through came from inside yourself. Mine came from outside. My
brother must have known he was likely to die before I got back,
but he also knew how much I'd set my heart on being selected to
come here, and he encouraged me and I made it and then, literally
within minutes before learning he was dead, I was told that the only
thing which might have compensated—being able to carry on with
the work he too wanted to see done—hung in the balance and might
be snatched away. The fact that it wasn't is due to you, because instead of being mealymouthed and servile and cautious like the rest

of us, you stood up to the general and let your real feelings show. You have a passionate commitment that I envy."

"But . . ." Ian sounded dazed. "But I remember clearly, when you sat down to weep for your brother, I was wishing I could feel so deeply. I can't. I don't have any passion in me."

She gazed at him searchingly. After a pause she said, "Is that true? I doubt it. I think it's more that you've never had anybody to feel passionately about."

"I . . ." Ian shook back his untidy hair and squared his shoulders. "I guess it could be."

"No family?"

"I was an only child, and orphaned young," he muttered.

"That accounts for a lot. But don't imagine you lack the capacity for deep feeling. You've demonstrated that it's there, even though it may be a trifle stunted. Unless you have any convincing objection, I propose to thank you for it in the nicest possible way. Lock the door and come here."

After a long time that passed in a flash, she stirred in near darkness and looked at her watch, which she had kept on.

"Let's go and join the party," she said. "The ship is due to leave at dawn, and after that we shall have more work than we can handle. Come on and make your good-byes."

Stretching like a satisfied cat, incredibly relaxed, smiling as though the muscles of his face had forgotten how to do anything else, Ian said, "Cathy, why—uh—why not somebody already?"

"What? Oh!" She shrugged, her dark hair loose around her creamy bare shoulders. "Well, naturally: several already. Ruggiero, Olaf before he became involved with Sue, even—after a lot of hard work— Igor. . . . But there's so much else to think about, and we're not here as settlers, so we don't think in terms of one-to-one relationships. Besides, there's never been anybody here to whom I felt I could grow close."

"You think you could to me? But you scarcely know me."

"I know you better than I did an hour ago, and I like what I've found out. I think you're the sort of person I can go on getting to know better and better for a long time. Which is a fair summary of what I've always told myself I wanted." She patted his arm affectionately. "Let's move. I don't suppose anyone is wondering where we are, but if you don't show up at all, they may get worried."

Next morning, when the *Stellaris* lofted skywards with that strange faint hum he had been told about, but of course had never heard—that vibration which made the very fabric of space seem to buzz with controlled gravitic energy—she stood at his side, fingers linked with his, and seemed to share the strange, rather shy pride which was burgeoning in his mind, pride that held out the lure of such hope as might make even the most vaulting ambition take on the promise of eventual reality.

IX

Cathy's prediction had been all too literal. From the day of the ship's departure onwards, he did indeed have more work than he could cope with.

If only I could have some other brilliant insights now and then, to keep my spirits up . . . !
But they didn't materialise. That wild guess about the weather-prediction machine remained unique and—worse, but unavoidably —seemed less memorable as the days leaked away. True, programming the computers with every known item of data concerning meteorological instruments did produce a very wide assortment of brand-new hypotheses. But that was what they remained. Not one translated into a certainty.
And for all we can tell it may have had nothing to do with weather after all. Given a simple physical principle—no matter what, magnetism, atmospheric pressure, refraction, anything—one can work outward from it along countless divergent paths. Maybe that bob-hanging-on-frame arrangement wasn't a tool or an instrument; maybe, in their view, it was a religious symbol or a work of art!
"Occam," he kept saying to himself grimly. "Remember the Razor: Don't multiply entities beyond necessity!"
But who could say what the lost natives had regarded as necessary?

A pattern of living and working had evolved since the foundation of the base which he readily adapted to. One thought in terms —effectively—of months, but they were formally termed "Progress Assessment Units." Each numbered thirty days, of which two at the beginning were spent on travel, to the outlying digs; then twenty were spent at the actual sites; then two more were allotted for a return to base; and three days of intensive conferences with the entire staff were topped off with three days of free time, which, so far as most people were concerned, meant constant debate, an informal continuation of the conferences. To prevent strain building up to the point where people might become stale, ill-tempered or obsessional, Rorschach had decreed years ago that the middle day of these last three would be the one on which nobody, but *nobody*, talked shop. In the morning and afternoon there were generally competitions; chess, go, athletics, darts, gymnastics, bridge and half a dozen other pastimes were selected on the basis of a computer-generated random-number list. And in the evening there was a party.

It was a well-balanced pattern. Given that the people here were dedicated volunteers totally committed to the work in hand, it would have been difficult to make them relax more frequently. The twenty-day periods of absolute unrelieved hard work typically generated just a fraction more mental activity than could be digested in the three-day conference period, and the "month-end" relaxation slot was just about long enough for them to unwind without losing sight of what they had been on the point of doing next.

Proof that the system was succeeding lay in the fact that even though thirty highly intelligent, highly individualistic experts were isolated here nineteen light-years from Earth with the most baffling possible problem, there had never been a feud, or any faction-forming, or any disagreement that came to blows. There were, inevitably, differences of opinion about precedence and priorities, because the available resources were so limited; these, though, fell into the category that might be called "schools of thought" rather than any real rift among the personnel.

Perhaps, Ian thought, living in the shadow of a thousand centuries of renewedly mindless evolution—as though the emergence of intelligent creatures here had been a mistake, a disturbance of the natural order, which now was restored—had made these people more careful about the use they made of their precious talent: reason.

Affable, stimulating, with a phenomenal grasp on the over-all pattern of what had been found here, Igor Andrevski took him on a tour of the major sites as a first move. At the site code-named Peat, Cathy was uncovering little by little the traces left by perhaps a couple of million natives: each a thinking being, each astonishingly imaginative. . . . Well, it went without saying. Had they not been like that, they could never have made such progress in so short a time.

And at Ash, Olaf and Sue were shifting thousands of tons of volcanic debris, revealing a very similar city but differently coloured: grey-white, where Peat was yellow-brown. The problems were similar, though. At Peat, biological action had rotted many of the buried artefacts before they were flooded by water that became stagnant and oxygen-free, giving rise to conditions like those which, back on Earth, had preserved the famous corpse of Tollund Man. At Ash, the heat of the falling volcanic ejecta had dehydrated the relics, but that had not been until hundreds of years after they began to rot.

Moreover the design, the layout, of the city was also similar. It was similar at the site named Silt, too, where Ruggiero and his helper were probing what might have become a bed of sandstone had a crustal plate not tilted as well as slipping when it accommodated with its neighbour, so that what might have been expected to disappear below sea level arched back up again to compensate for a sudden nose dive a hundred kilometres away.

And there was Seabed, which they visited in aqualungs, where gorgeously coloured weed floated in the microclimate of the currents caused by the encrusted streets and roadways because they were transverse to the tides here, and weird purple animals bombarded them with stinging but harmless jets of a substance which could kill many native fish.

And again the pattern was similar at Snowfall One, bar some

minor changes which could easily be due to climatic conditions. And . . .

Late one night, in the cosy comfort of the awning which they had extended from the side of their hovercraft, with a bitter wind outside and the savoury aroma of the food delivered by their portable processor rich within, Ian said suddenly to Igor, "One of each. And only one of each."

Igor glanced at him, his expression serious. "Yes. I find it incredible, and I suspect you do, too. Amplify."

"Well . . ." Ian hesitated. "Could any intelligent species be so easily bored that having done a thing once that would be its limit?"

"Tell me what you think. I've been here more than four years. I'd welcome your fresh approach."

"I think not," Ian said. "Unless—and this is crucial—unless they had such a perfect grasp of potential, unless they had such vivid imaginations, in other words, that they preferred insight to experiment."

"But where in the universe can you start from that will permit you to do that?" Igor slapped his thigh. "There are phenomena on phenomena. You *cannot* extrapolate from the macro to the micro, and I don't care what anybody says. If these creatures possessed a sense which detected electromagnetic fields (and we hold that they did because that's the path evolution has followed in other cases), then I don't see how that can have taken them any more directly to the concept of energy and mass as interchangeable than—than our sense of hearing led us to the barometer or the altimeter or the vacuum pump, even though those all relate to the same environmental medium which conveys sound. And yet the fact stands: They appear to have invented the city *once*, and at every site we've dug over we find precisely the same pattern, modified only insofar as we move farther and farther away from the centre. I *wish* our computers would tell us whether that centre is more likely to have been Ash than Peat! My money is on Ash—but what we take for simple and primitive utensils and tools may, on the contrary, have been sophisticated final versions of things that began as something far more complicated! Compare a vacuum-tube radio set with its modern counterpart, completely solid-state and grown rather than manufactured because in effect it consists of three crystal-diffusion units, very carefully doped and very carefully imprinted."

Ian gave a thoughtful nod, mentally reviewing the pattern of cultural diffusion which was in its way analogous to the crystalline-diffusion process Igor had just mentioned.

"Every city," he said at length, "has all the most advanced features: at the centre, a complex of some kind which includes what you've baptised a library, plus large halls, and open spaces which probably correspond to a square or marketplace in human terms. Good. *But* it isn't a simple matter of this particular pattern suiting a particular kind of creature—more, it's a matter of this creature having invented a pattern and got it right the first time, so that whenever a new city was created the former pattern was modified in only the most minor details."

"And some cities, which by both geographical proximity and the associated relics we can term the oldest, have those modifications as indisputable later additions. . . . Hmm!" Igor snapped his fingers. "I just thought of the *Stellaris!*"

Ian looked at him with respect. "I get the point," he breathed. "After every trip, a change derived from recent experience. . . . But—but damn it! I find it just as hard to believe in a creature which learned that quickly from experience, and thought it worth applying the knowledge straightaway, as I do to believe in a species that never bothered to experiment and always got everything right at once!"

"Yet that's what we've run into!" Igor said savagely. "*One* aircraft, for example"—he gestured with his thumb over his shoulder towards the Snowfall One site where the craft had been discovered —"when it's definite that they had fast long-distance communications for a long time. Why not dozens of them? Were they all broken up for scrap and salvage during a period of decline so brief we haven't been able to tap into proof of it?"

"*One* oceangoing ship," Ian concurred. "Which is even more extraordinary. Search the seabeds of Earth, and you'd come upon scores, hundreds of fairly well preserved wrecks. And in a period of decline—which I grant you is a strong possibility—how would they have been able to dredge the ocean floor for salvageable gear?"

"Exactly. That takes considerable technology." Igor shook his head, his expression lugubrious. "And where did they launch their moonships from? We've never found even the counterpart of an airport, let alone a Cape Kennedy or a Baikonur or a Woomera!"

"I can see only one explanation," Ian said after a pause during which he listened to the wind howling in the nearby mountains.

Igor brightened. "You see even one possibility? Share it with me!"

"That by our standards just about every member of the species was a genius and could undertake calculations as a matter of routine which we'd find so tiresome we'd have to hand them over to computers."

Igor thought about that for a while, and finally nodded.

"It's a valid insight, that. At any rate I think so. I can sense a lot of implications fanning out from it, as I'm sure you can. It would lead at once to the success of virtually every new invention they came up with. Is that what you mean?"

"Mm-hm." Ian rubbed his chin. "It would explain why only one ship can be found sunk; the second time, they got it so right that for as long as they used ocean transport they never had another wreck. It might even explain why there are no airports or moon-rocket launch bases."

Igor blinked at him. "I'm not sure I see quite how—"

"Because they went for the maximum return on minimum effort every time," Ian broke in. "Rather than waste time and energy on ancillary systems, they made everything self-contained and self-supporting. That flying machine: didn't Ruggiero say point-blank that it was capable of vertical takeoff?"

"Yes, and I think he's proved it. You know it was pretty badly crushed, as what wouldn't be after millennia buried in a moving glacier? But all the computerised reconstructions he's developed for it agree on exactly that point: it had landing gear adequate only for a direct descent onto flat level ground. It didn't roll or taxi; it squatted."

Ian gave a faint smile. "Yes, I've been spending a lot of my time since I arrived reviewing data of that kind. I was very struck by the points Ruggiero has made concerning the identifiable relics of advanced technology . . . not that there are very many, are there?"

"Maybe we'd be worse off if there were?"

"That's a painful but significant argument." Ian pantomimed an exaggerated wince, as though he had been stabbed in the heart.

"Yes, except . . . Never mind; I didn't mean to interrupt. I think you were going to say something else."

Ian hesitated. He said at length, "Yes, but a point has suddenly struck me which I think I was blind to overlook before. Igor!" He hunched forward, gazing at the older man. "Was it when you realised there really *was* only one of everything here that you decided it would be worth asking for the help of someone like me?"

"Of course. If it weren't for that, a palaeolinguist would be no more help here than—than a blacksmith. So long as we imagined they were very like us indeed, we assumed there must have been dozens, perhaps hundreds, of different languages. There's an excellent chance, based on our recent discoveries, that language too may have been invented once on this planet, and evolved but never developed into the range of separate families you find on Earth. My knowledge of linguistic evolution is sketchy, but I fancy something of the sort happened in China. Isn't it true that over a period of a millennium or so the spoken language there changed radically, but the written language remained comprehensible?"

Ian nodded, focussing his eyes on nowhere. "And particularly in view of the fact that they very likely imprinted their 'inscriptions' directly, so that language consisted of shared patterns of nervous impulses common to all individuals—in other words, they probably didn't use names because they identified themselves by simply being!" He sat upright with a jerk.

"Hey! Now, *that's* a point! In a sense, maybe this species never stopped talking! Because so long as they were alive, they were interacting one with every other! Igor, I'm obliged. You just gave me a hell of a good takeoff run!"

X

Outside, as ever, the sun beat fiercely down, but in the relic shed it was cool and the light was filtered through tinted windows. Ian sat at the bench facing the computer remote, double-checking the catalogue numbers of a dozen objects ranged to his left: the palm-sized, finger-thick blocks of artificial crystal which the aliens had imprinted with microvolt currents, an eon ago, and which still betrayed at least a hint of the information-bearing pattern frozen into their molecular structure.

Before him was a modification of a device which was used at the digs to detect the presence of magnetised materials, a cradlelike frame connected to a series of meters and thence to the computers.

Behind him the door opened. He ignored it; today was the day after the end of the work period, and people were bound to be bringing in newly discovered artefacts, but he had particularly requested that any further "libraries" be left undisturbed so that in due course he could apply his embryo theories to them.

Then a light hand stroked his cheek and a voice murmured close to his ear, "Had a good month?"

He almost dropped the crystal whose number he was verifying.

"Cathy!" he exclaimed, and hugged her around the waist. "Yes—yes, I think I have had a good month."

"What are you doing?"

"Making some extra calibrations of the patterns printed in these things. Looking for a time dimension, mainly—because if there isn't a progression from beginning to end, an element of sequentiality, we shall almost certainly never understand their language."

"Sort of like trying to figure out whether a human book was read this way up from left to right, or the other way up from right to left?"

"Absolutely the same sort of problem."

She perched on the side of the bench at his right, long legs swinging, the zipper of her blouse drawn far down on her bosom for the heat.

"I think it's a miracle you can conceive a way of reading their language at all," she said after a pause.

"If we do, it will be," Ian sighed. "But Igor gave me a fascinating insight which suggested a potential lead. Back on Earth, when I was first introduced to the idea that these blocks might be inscribed with a counterpart of writing, I immediately assumed pens, styli, typewriters, whatever the hell."

"No tools?" Cathy said sharply.

"No tools. Because since it's been shown that some of the surviving species can print rocks directly with a magnetic trace, we've been able to consider the most interesting possibility of all: that they didn't have to invent writing—they evolved it. It was as natural to them as making mouth noises is to us. They merely refined and improved the materials. Instead of making do with chunks of rock, they manufactured an ideal variety of crystal. Here it is." He waved at the array beside him on the bench.

"And that means their writing was more like the groove on a disc record or the pattern on a tape." Cathy nodded. "With the bonus effect that they could read it back directly."

"It goes even deeper. They didn't have to invent a system of sound-to-symbol correspondence. Their symbols were a direct reflection of a real-time process going on in their nervous systems; in other words, they experienced the imprinted pattern as though it were being—ah—spoken to them. That is, assuming this electromagnetic sense was what they used where we'd use sound, and all the indications point that way. I asked Lucas to make sure that next time his people are studying a colony of animals, they should measure the changing electrical fields as well as merely observing."

Cathy raised her eyebrows. "Ve-ery interesting! I can see another consequence you haven't mentioned."

"What?"

"Well . . . how could they tell lies?"

Ian whistled. "That's a point, isn't it? I hadn't got that far. You're probably right. I don't see how they could be dishonest with each other. . . . Hmm! Do you suppose that's why they got from nowhere to the moon in such a hurry?"

And before she could answer, he snapped his fingers. "Yet they must have had some kind of nonreal mode of—of speech. If communication were limited to actual experience and present mental state, it couldn't include hypotheses."

"But couldn't they be labelled?" Cathy suggested. "I mean . . . Well, under most normal circumstances a human being can distinguish between what's remembered and what's imagined. Maybe the same sort of overtones were involved in their communication."

"M-m-mm . . ." Ian plucked at his chin; he had decided to let his beard grow out, but as yet it was sparse. "I think you're on to something. I'll check it out when I have the time. For the moment, if you'll excuse me, I have to finish calibrating these; I meant to get them out of the way last night, but I ran into a snag."

"What exactly are you looking for?" Cathy said. "Apart from the temporal sequence you mentioned. What starting point can there be in the case of a nonhuman language?"

Ian gave a humourless chuckle. "Now, that's a good question, if you like! Basically, patterns that repeat in similar contexts. I'll show you."

He picked up the nearest crystal, laid it in his cradle and pushed a switch. At once, on the big screen above which was linked to the main computers, a complex stable pattern appeared somewhat resembling a transform of the sounds made by a full symphony orchestra, in seven colours.

"Those colours correspond to levels of impregnation," he explained. "Not physical levels—degrees of intensity. Of course I can go to physical parameters, too." He touched another switch, and the colour distribution altered instantly, though the basic form of the display remained the same.

"And I can go arbitrarily to various temporal parameters—read in sequence from left to right, up to down, this face to the farther one. . . . Topologically speaking, though, reading all the crystals in the same orientation should produce a sufficient degree of invariance to determine whether any patterns which repeat are isolable as the equivalent of phonemic units."

"Uh . . ." She shook her head. "You just lost me."

"Well, suppose when I've finished calibrating every crystal found at one particular site—which will take quite a while until I figure out an optimum configuration to automate the process with—suppose I find there's a pattern which can be isolated in every single block . . . which actually is too much to hope for, so I'd set the machines to determine what patterns occur on the n-plus level, in other words what patterns have been found more often than once per crystal. Then I'd sift those, looking for the one which occurred literally *the* most often, and make an assumption about it."

"Such as?"

"First of all, that it was a statement concerning an individual member of the species. The equivalent in human terms would be 'he is,' 'she did,' 'they were'—that kind of thing. And then I'd look for associative correspondences, or rather I'd programme the computers to do that. I'd look for a phrase of the structure 'he is XYZ' which I could match up with another 'they are XYZ.' And then I'd cross-match all those with other phrases of the same general form. You see, I'm looking not for a translation, which would be ridiculous, but for a grammar. Once we have a grammar, the rest can be filled in by trial and error."

Somewhat doubtfully she said, "Do you mean by 'grammar' what they taught me at school?"

"Oh, no. Not unless you were very lucky. Where were you educated?"

"Partly in Dublin and partly in Athens."

"Ouch!" Ian threw up his hands. "In that case it's a miracle you found your way here—if you asked me to name two really reactionary centres of linguistic teaching, stuck in the mud of the classical languages even after generations of fresh insight after fresh insight into what language is really doing . . . Excuse me; that's a bit of a hobbyhorse of mine. But you weren't selected to come here for your brilliance in linguistics, so . . ." He interrupted himself, falling over his tongue. "Oh, sometimes I think I'm the most tactless person alive! I mean, I know all about your work with Soper and Dupont at the Viking sites in Nova Scotia—"

"Actually what settled the matter was the colour of my eyes," she snapped. "Idiot!" And blew him a kiss, and added, "Go *on*, will you?"

"Uh . . . Sure. A grammar is not what I suspect was taught to you: a set of rules which lays down that this is right and this is wrong and this is a solecism but permissible—hm?" He tousled his hair with distracted fingers. "No, it's far more like a system of topological relationships, and in fact modern grammar borrows much of its terminology, like invariance, straight from topology. To give an example: It's not a question of 'if member-class-A then member-class-B'—nothing to do with 'the adjective agrees with the noun in gender, number and case'—but much more like 'if member-class-B then member-class-A already happened provided A and B are members of the same field.' Kind of a feedback situation!"

"I think I follow." Frowning. "But even assuming that this is true of human languages, what grounds do you have to imagine it may be true of the native languages?"

"Well, Igor's insight suggested that they may not have had *languages*, plural, but at worst the equivalent of dialects . . . which would be a logical starting point anywhere in the universe, come to think of it. It's been shown that all human languages have a fundamentally identical structure—"

"*What?*"

Ian looked faintly surprised. "What else would you expect, given that we all go on two legs, all make noises with a mouth in the front of the head, and so on? The fundamental structure is associative; juxtaposition and sequence in time are a perfect instance of invariance in the grammatical sense. You make a statement about event A and object B by composing an utterance that connects the agreed sound symbol of each with the other. If a language can be called a language, then it's got to have at least that intrinsic feature, regardless of the decorations added later. You surely must have been told that baby talk in every known human language is grammatically consistent?"

She shook her head, seeming a little dazed.

"Well, it's true. A Japanese mother and a German mother and a Russian mother and a Maori mother will all use the same kind of grammar when teaching their babies to talk: the very simple two-unit pattern which was what you and I and every other articulate person began with."

Still apparently a trifle dubious, Cathy nonetheless nodded. "Even so, if you establish this kind of pattern, how far has that taken you? I mean, where do you start the actual translation, which is what it's all about?"

Ian leaned back with a sigh. "Oh, once we've got past the initial stage of analysis, it'll be a bit like what Ventris did with Linear B, except he did have some known languages to work from. . . ."

"Details!"

"I'll show you where to track them down in the computers. The story's quite fascinating, a real piece of detective work. It turned out that what he had, even though everyone else said it couldn't be, was archaic Greek, written in a script meant for a totally different kind of language. And you ought to look at the way the Spanish priests misread the writing of the Amerinds, too, because the only script they knew was phonetic—more or less—and they had no vaguest notion of what a hieroglyphic syllabary was like." He sighed again, more heavily.

"Ian dear!" She leaned towards him. "I don't want to be told about your problems. I can imagine them. I want to be told about your ways of solving them!"

"Sorry!" He pulled himself together and essayed a not too successful laugh.

"Well!" he resumed. "The next stage is to apply some *a priori* assumptions. Igor mentioned one of the most important when we were having that initial confrontation with Ordoñez-Vico. Most, though not all, human languages differentiate between masculine and feminine, in noun and pronoun structure particularly. Though of course a great many languages extend the concept of gender far beyond anything found in European languages. So a good point to start would be to look for structural differentiation that might conceivably correspond with the sex change of the natives. It may not work; we may not come up with anything as simple as 'he does XYZ' versus 'she does XYZ' because the—the word units may be absolutely different for the active male phase and the sedentary female stage. As it were, 'he eats' might turn into 'she devours.' But the principle is the only one we have, so if a hunt for sexual indicators fails, we'll have to carry on eliminating all the possibilities in succession. It goes without saying that a creature like what we find here must breathe, eat, excrete, relate to its fellows, communicate, and so on. So we'll have to sieve out any such word units and test them for consistency and invariance."

He glanced at the crystal before him. "Oh, that's been in there long enough!" he said, and removed it and reached for another. Craning forward to look at the screen as he did so, Cathy exclaimed, "Say, when you touched it, the pattern altered!"

"Well, of course." Ian blinked at her. "I'm a conductor, and so are you."

"No, that's not what I mean." She slipped down from the bench. "It was more like . . . No, I'm sure those metres jumped. Have you checked the crystals for a piezo effect?"

Ian sat rock-still for a second. Then he grabbed her hand and bestowed a smacking kiss on the palm.

"Genius!"

"What?"

"There's an old saying: The genius sees what happens, but the plodder sees what he expects to happen. Ay-ay-*ay!* Even if this does mean I have to recalibrate every single damn' crystal, I think what you just did was tell me how to locate the time dimension. Hang on!"

He dropped the crystal back in the cradle, and this time, instead of letting it lie there, pressed on it, at first gently and then with increasing force until the pattern on the screen dissolved into a blur.

"That's it!" he shouted. "Cathy, you're wonderful!"

XI

"Director! May I talk to you for a moment?"

Strolling around the perimeter of the base as twilight fell, Valentine Rorschach didn't pause as Ian called from the window of the relic shed.

"Provided you quit addressing me so formally!" he answered. "Come out here and walk with me for a while. You spend too much time cooped up in there!"

A minute later, puffing from having come at a dead run, Ian fell into step beside him. He said anxiously, "I hope I didn't interrupt, but—"

Rorschach did exactly that, with malice aforethought.

"You're driving yourself too hard, Ian. I hate to say so, but I've seen it happen before and I don't want to have to order Lucas to start issuing you with tranquilizers. You lack perspective, man! You've achieved more within a shorter time of your arrival than anyone since the base was established, at least in terms of generating new ideas for us to follow up. Why is that not enough for you? Is it because you're afraid of losing Cathy if you don't outstrip all possible competition?"

Ian was taken totally aback by the question. He stopped in his tracks, and Rorschach likewise halted, swinging to face him.

"Ian, Ian—*Ian*. . . . You knew pretty much what I was going to be like before you came here, didn't you?"

Ian nodded. Part of the preparation for his trip, and indeed part of the briefings for everybody due to replace the personnel rotated home, had consisted in face-to-face no-exit confrontations with clever actors taught to duplicate members of the staff here, so that the newcomers would be acquainted with their failings as well as their virtues, and any dangerous weaknesses on their own side would be revealed.

"Well, I imagine they covered everything except this new baldness of mine," Rorschach went on, tapping his over-high forehead. "Equally, they took you to little bits, you know, and they warned me in the tapes that arrived with you that you were liable to overcommit yourself. So . . . Let me put it this way: I'm delighted you called out to me, and that we're talking out of earshot of everybody else, because otherwise I'd have had to contrive some elaborate excuse to have a private chat."

Ian blinked at him.

"Oh, not to issue any kind of—of reprimand!" Rorschach beat the air as though it had annoyed him. "Just to warn you that you're overdoing it, and there's no need."

Licking his lips, Ian looked around, taking in the now distant shapes of the base buildings, the long shadows left on the glass foundation beneath by the sun as it sank below the horizon in a welter of thinly shredded cloud . . . and said at length, "You know, for a moment I was going to be angry at having my privacy invaded. But it wouldn't make sense, would it, to prize privacy when we're trying to peel away all the veils of history from the native race?"

"When you're provoked into it," Rorschach said in a judicious tone, "you're capable of admirable insight. I don't mean on the professional level; you've demonstrated that beyond a doubt, and in fact I've complimented Igor on his insight in nominating you for recruitment. No, I'm thinking rather of . . ." He turned and gazed towards the setting sun.

"I'm thinking of the point I touched on just now: having to run to keep up. Agreed, it would be marvelous if we could solve the mystery of the aliens before the ship comes back. But what can we do here that will decide whether or not it does return?"

The words struck a chill deep into Ian's mind. After a pause for sober reflection, he said, "Do you honestly think they may not send her back?"

Rorschach spread his hands in an empty gesture. "It's one of the possibilities I have to bear in mind as director of the base. That's all. Oh—no, it isn't quite all. I was going to make a point in connection with you and Cathy."

"What?"

"Over the years since I was appointed, I've done my best to devalue all the things that got in the way of our thinking at home. High on the list is jealousy, of course. Did it ever strike you that it's most corrosive when it occurs in what might otherwise have been a stable relationship, immune from outside interference? Don't bother to answer; as I said, when you're pushed to it, you possess admirable insight. But someone has to push, and I'm pushing, and what I mean is that Cathy had been here two years already when you arrived, and at the present moment nobody resents the fact that she decided it was with you she wanted to establish a permanent relationship—small wonder, since you're so talented—but the situation is precarious and if the suspicion burgeons in one single mind that you're driving yourself because you're afraid Cathy can be seduced away from you, instead of because you want to solve the mystery that concerns us all . . . I believe there's no need to labour the point."

Ian remained silent for a long moment. He said eventually, "Valentine, now I know what made you such an ideal choice as director here. I never met anybody more tactful than you. I'll postpone the request I was going to make."

Rorschach chuckled. "Go ahead and make it anyway," he said. "The answer will be no, but I'd like to have the data on file, as it were, so as not to be taken by surprise."

"Okay," Ian said. He drew up the zipper of his blouse because it was turning cool with the advent of evening, and absently began to walk again, Rorschach keeping pace. Gazing down at the ground, he went on, "I was thinking of something which, I suppose, tipped the balance between success and failure for me when I was working on the Zimbabwe ruins."

"When you proved that what might have been simple decoration was actually a script," Rorschach said.

"Mm-hm." Ian nodded; it wasn't worth pretending to be modest about that, because if he hadn't done so he would not have come to Igor's attention and would not have been invited here. "I decided that before I could assign any—any levels of priority to the various possible significances of the script, if it was one, I'd have to think myself into the skin of the man who made the inscription. So for a month I lived as he would have done: eating what I could trap or gather, sleeping rough every night, drinking from water holes shared by animals and hoping that I'd live through the infections I was bound to fall sick with. . . . I stripped myself, little by little, of the ideas I'd brought with me, and climbed back towards the basics, hunger and thirst and heat and cold and dark and light. I got one hell of a bad case of sunburn. But I also got what I'd set out to look for: an insight into the man who inscribed those mysterious symbols."

Rorschach uttered an unashamed whistle of astonishment. "You want to try that here? But how can any human possibly dream of establishing a sense of identity with the Draconians?"

Ian stroked his newly luxuriant beard with a lugubrious scowl.

"He can't" was his answer. "On the other hand, he can struggle his way towards a sense of what for them was reality. We see colour, for instance; presumably, so did they because there are eyelike organs on all the large species here. But was colour important to them? I suspect not. I suspect that what we would think of as tone colour—in other words, the subjective response they had to the *pitch* of an electromagnetic field—must have been what counted for them. I don't know, I can't be sure, but I'd bet on it."

"Even assuming that that's so," Rorschach said after a pause for reflection, "are you asking me—or rather, if I hadn't declined in advance, would you be asking me—for permission to set up house in one of the native city-sites, and try to live off the land, as it were, until you achieved some kind of divine revelation?" He chuckled. "Hunger and thirst and subclinical infection, you know, generate the most surprising attitudes towards the universe, but I doubt whether many of them are valid!"

"Not exactly," Ian said awkwardly. "What I was actually going to ask for was the resources to start constructing a simulacrum of one of the natives."

They had been strolling along side by side. Now, without warning, Rorschach stopped as though he had struck a glass wall.

"Say that again slowly," he requested. "And let me have the full details."

"Well—ah . . ." Ian made vague waving movements. "What I was thinking of was a sort of shell, about the right size for a man to fit into, with the necessary movements built in, based on the kind of principle they use for modern prosthetics. I imagine the data to design a gadget of that type must be in store here because the medical data banks are very comprehensive, aren't they? In effect one would need to feel directly the actual bodily processes of the alien creature. Whether it could be carried as far as the crucial sexual switch, from active male to sedentary female, I don't know, but there could be ways of faking that, I guess. And just so long as the—the world view was right. . . . For example, suppose one devalued sight to plain black and white but upgraded sound, using a sonar unit, to the point where that combined with enhanced tactility was providing a majority of the user's information about the environment . . . and assigned additional variety to suggest the range of electromagnetic perceptions we presume these creatures had, and . . ." He clawed the air, seeming to grope for the right words. "And as for the hormonal revolution—well, one doesn't have to be a woman to find analogies to the process of pregnancy and labour, even though one does have to throw out a hell of a lot of in-built biases."

He hesitated. "*Would* that be permissible?" he ventured.

"Not only would it be, it is!" Rorschach declared with an air of finality. "In fact, I think I can suggest a means of converting the tactile impulses into something more significant to the user. If one were to exploit the known sensitivity of the retina to changing magnetic fields, one might very well—but damn it!" He rounded on Ian. "This is absurd!"

"I'm afraid I don't understand."

"No, you wouldn't. But I should have done. I could kick myself from here to—to the civil engineering block!" In lieu of which Rorschach stamped on the glassy ground. "Yes, yes, *yes!* The technology exists for us to get under the skin of another species, and so far as I'm aware it's never been tried! Are we mad? Are we out of our minds?"

"If you really want an answer, and that question isn't simply rhetorical . . . ?"

"What? Yes indeed, I do want an answer!" Rorschach's voice had peaked to a near shout; now it abruptly dropped to normal. "Quite seriously, Ian, a project like yours has been feasible since long before we arrived. The techniques exist, or can be developed from the kind of gadgetry we use to help the blind, the maimed, the deaf. . . . Lord, that lie detector of Ordoñez-Vico's has a sense that most human beings don't possess, because it can analyse our body secretions and compare them with a norm and then compare the norm with the profile of the speaker's voice. If we do have that gift, it's a long way below the conscious level."

Ian was shaking his head over and over. "No, you're jumping to conclusions, I'm afraid. The real point is this. Not until we had a clear grasp of how different the natives were from us, rather than how much alike we were, could anybody—me, or Igor, or you, anybody—have suggested this plan. Because if it works, what will count is not how much of the aliens we can afterwards understand; it's what they might have understood of us if they'd survived to meet us face to face."

Face strained and anxious in the gathering dusk, he leaned close to Rorschach as though half afraid he wasn't making himself clear.

"You're absolutely correct," the director said. "And so was Igor when he suggested that we ask for you. You've just put into words —more, into the shape of a practicable plan—something which I've sensed, just as I'm sure Igor must have . . . and done nothing about. Because we couldn't see any way of implementing it."

He slapped Ian on the shoulder.

"I think this month I may break one of my own rules. I think we may talk shop on the day when it's forbidden. At any rate, if I know my staff, I can foresee this proposition of yours sparking their imaginations like a light being set to a blasting fuse!"

XII

Sitting informally around in the refectory, some of them sipping wine or beer or excellent imitations of fruit juice, the staff listened to the regular bald summary reports with which the monthly conferences always commenced. After hearing the others out and making his own brief report, Rorschach called on Ian to describe his new idea.

Igor and Cathy had already been told about it and made prompt, excited suggestions, but the impact on everybody else was stunning. When he finished speaking, there was a long thoughtful silence; then, one after another, people started to nod, gazing into nowhere.

"I think it has something for all of us," Rorschach said at length. "I can see dozens of ways in which it can be expected to generate spin-off in the form of brand-new insights. Let's sort out one urgent question first, though. Karen, can it be done?"

The plump civil engineer was leaning back in her chair with a dreamy, speculative expression. At mention of her name she roused herself.

"Hm? Oh, sorry, Valentine. . . . Yes, I can't think of any reason why not. Though it does depend on how elaborate you want to make the—ah—the sensory illusions."

Lucas Wong leaned forward. The short, heavy-set medical biologist, half American and half Chinese, took more after his father's than his mother's traditions, and seldom spoke without long reflection on any weighty matter. Now he was uncharacteristically enthusiastic.

"Oh, there may be ways we can get around the sensory problem!

Ian, do you know whether you're a suitable subject for hypnosis?"

Ian snapped his fingers. "No, I've never been tested for that, but aren't there drugs which can be employed to make one more susceptible?"

"I'll check that out," Lucas promised, and rubbed his hands in obvious glee. "Oh, this is a marvelous idea, it really is!"

"We'll have to build the simulacrum oversize," Nadine Shah warned. "Fitting a man inside it—hmm! But as to the actual construction, I think that will be quite easy. I'm certain we have sufficient data in store about the physical properties of native tissue, the articulation of joints and the characteristics of their nervous system. Achmed, what about the interface between the machine and Ian himself?"

"No problem there," Achmed answered. "Particularly if he can be hypnotised. We can use microminiaturised sensors with some kind of direct nervous input, the same as they use on mechanical arms and legs nowadays. I'm sure details of those must be in store in the medical banks."

Ruggiero Bono caught Rorschach's eye. "Valentine, can I ask a question? It may seem trivial, but . . . Ian, what exactly are you expecting to get out of this gadget? I agree it's a fascinating project and certainly will jar us into thinking about problems that might not otherwise occur to us—but let's face it, a man isn't a Draconian and never can be!"

"You heard in Igor's report that, thanks to Cathy, I discovered how the natives most probably read their printed crystals, manually deforming them to amplify the otherwise very faint patterns. The trouble is this." Ian looked rueful. "Precisely because of the piezo effect structured into them, the simple weight of the overlay at the various sites where we've found libraries has dreadfully distorted what trace patterns remain. It is in fact amazing that we've managed to find so many well-preserved crystals."

He spread his hands.

"The consequence, of course, is that instead of immediately becoming easier, as I hoped, my job has suddenly proved to be more difficult than it seemed before. And it won't ever stand a hope of getting done unless I can grope my way to an educated guess about the reason why Draconians used these crystals. Cathy has correctly pointed out that it's unlikely they were able to lie to one another—"

"Why not?" Sue Tennant demanded. He gave a summary of the thinking that lay behind the assumption, and she rounded her mouth into an O and leaned back in her chair, convinced.

He went on, "So it's improbable that we have to deal with fiction, isn't it? On the other hand: they had advanced science, so there may be the equivalent of textbooks in the libraries. And they had a keen sense of aesthetics, symmetry, proportion and natural rhythms; a glance at the map of one of their cities will confirm that. So the crystals may well be works of art, counterparts of music or poetry. If that's the case, we shall never be able to do more than we can with them already: amplify and display the patterns stored in them.

"There's one ray of hope, though. Stop and think for a moment about the communication pattern of a creature that's constantly aware of a changing, pulsing, vibrating aura, to which every other member of the species contributes simply by existing. Would their language not depend on referents to real-time events rather than arbitrary symbols like human words? Let me give an example of what I mean. Individual A wants to inquire whether Individual B is hungry. Does he generate a completely unrelated pattern of signals? I say to someone, 'Would you like something to eat?' There is nothing of the nature of food or hunger in the question, is there? But a Draconian would—at least I suspect he would—ask by imitating the pattern associated with lack of food, and modulate it by imposing other patterns defining 'ask' and direct what he was saying to the correct hearer by reflecting that other person's pattern . . . as it were."

"They spoke in ideograms," Lucas Wong said, and snapped his fingers.

"Right! Right!" Growing more and more excited, Ian leapt from his chair and began to pace back and forth, frowning terribly. "I haven't managed to work it all out in my mind yet, but the outlines are starting to appear. Just as Chinese writing originally consisted of stylised pictograms, so the Draconian language would have evolved from a number of relatively simple root concepts most probably associated with bodily states. Naturally, over the centuries it would have grown to be tremendously sophisticated, and the same difficulty that a modern person finds in dissecting the original shape for 'man' or 'house' or 'sun' from a contemporary Chinese symbol will no doubt be found as we try to analyse these imprinted patterns. But we take it for granted that they did get hungry, feel tired, experience the sexual urge, and so on."

Ruggiero was nodding repeatedly. Now he said, "You've answered my question splendidly, only here's another. Even assuming you do manage to make your educated guess, and it turns out that we actually have—oh, let's be optimistic and say textbooks—how in the world are you going to extract any meaning from them? Trial and error could take from now until doomsday!"

"Not to mention," Achmed put in, "the fact that we now have thousands and thousands of these crystals, but the ones we most want may be the spoiled ones. If the Draconians did leave a message about their fate, in the faint hope that one day someone might come here and read it, they'd have made it conspicuous. Put it on their moon, for example. But we know that up there no crystals were found at all."

"I think they may have been more special than just books," Igor said musingly. He cupped his chin in his upturned hand, staring at the floor.

"How do you mean?" Rorschach said.

"Oh . . ." Igor waved in exasperation. "More like experience stores. Think how useful it would be to us if we could go somewhere and hear—perceive directly—read the thoughts of a long-dead genius. That would condense the time needed to climb from a primitive village to a moonship, wouldn't it?"

For an instant they sat dumbfounded at the grandiosity of the concept; then Achmed pulled a calculator from his pocket, passed his fingers rapidly over its input side and shook his head.

"Sorry, Igor. The idea's ingenious, but it won't work. The capacity is inadequate by a factor of several thousand. You'd just about manage to store two total personalities in a library of the size we've so far discovered."

"I think you'd be lucky to pack in two," Ian said.

Igor shrugged and sat back. "Pity!" he said with his usual engaging grin. "I thought I'd had a brilliant inspiration."

"In a way you have," Ian admitted. "Given direct experiential communication with other people, and total honesty, plus what we assume to have been extremely high intelligence by our standards . . . Nadine!"

The comparative biologist glanced at him. "Yes?"

"Those black shreds associated with the telescope, the bioelectronic system as we've decided to call it: are there any similar objects here on the planet itself?"

"Nothing we've been able to identify for sure," Nadine answered. "Which is hardly surprising. The stuff would have rotted or maybe been eaten!"

"Yes, I suppose so," Ian sighed.

Igor erupted again. "Eaten! Say, you don't suppose that any of the quasi-RNA has been transmitted down to the present, do you? Wasn't there something I once read about printed memory molecules . . . ?"

"For all we can tell," Nadine said, "we may already have seen direct descendants of the Draconians, never mind descendants of the creatures that ate their organic circuitry. Had that never struck you?"

Igor nodded. "Yes, I remember discussing that idea when I first arrived, on the trip before yours. You're thinking in terms of a harmful dominant mutation which deprived them of the power to reason and communicate?"

"If that were the explanation for their downfall," Lucas said, "after a hundred thousand years of mindless reproduction you'd have to regard the present-day offspring as a different species, surely."

"Agreed," Nadine said. "Still, the fact does stand that there are literally hundreds of surviving animals like enough to the Draconians to be their cousins. That is, assuming the scanty nature of the actual physical remains we've found is a reliable guide, and we haven't inadvertently filled out our picture of them by drawing too many comparisons with the contemporary fauna."

"In any case," Ian said flatly, "I don't see how such a mutation could have spread so rapidly through a species with such command of applied biology."

"Good point," Olaf Mukerji said. "It couldn't have, not unless it was spread deliberately, and that brings us clear back to the idea of warfare, or a decision to commit racial suicide. And when we get back to something we've talked about *ad nauseam*, it's high time to stop waffling and reach a decision. I formally move that Ian be given all the facilities he requires. I think the idea is admirable and I can imagine the results being sensational."

It was not, however, Ian who generated the next sensation.

Ten days into the next monthly work period, he was talking with Lucas Wong and Nadine Shah about some snags that had developed in the first design for the mock Draconian. Grouped around a computer display screen, they were testing the various analogies derived from surviving species which best promised to allow the occupant to inhabit the device in comfort. At the far end of the computer and communications hall Achmed Hossein was engaged in a routine series of checks of their satellite relay equipment.

The conversation was becoming heated; none of them noticed when Achmed broke off his work with an exclamation and bent to listen intently to one of the links connecting the base with the archeological digs.

But a few seconds later he called out and interrupted them.

"Hey! That was Cathy! She and Igor have found something incredible at the peat site!"

"What?" the other three demanded in unison.

"She says it's indescribable, but so tremendous we all ought to drop whatever we're doing and go there at once."

"Can't she send us a picture?" Ian asked.

"She says Igor is too excited to bother rigging the cameras, and anyway they want to strip off as much cover as they can before nightfall." Achmed reached for a switch and sent out a signal for Rorschach, who shortly answered over his personal communicator.

He made his mind up the moment he heard the news.

"If Igor says it's that remarkable, we pay attention. Pass the word. Is Lucas there? Ask if he'd mind being left alone here for a short while."

"I mind very much" was the reply. "But go ahead, and bring me some souvenirs when you come home."

They reached the peat site well before sunset, and the moment they breasted the adjacent hill over which the conveyors were carrying spoil, they realised just how accurate Igor's claim had been.

Now the huge pit was about ten metres deeper than when Ian had seen it for the first time; the digging machines were all concentrating on one small area near the centre.

Small by comparison with the full extent of the site, but not with a human being. Cathy and Igor were both dwarfed by the walls of the pit, and at its bottom . . .

Cathy caught sight of the new arrivals as they left their hovercraft and came hurrying down a slanting walkway from the pit's rim. She rushed to greet them, though Igor offered no more than a cheerful wave and a shout. Both were muddy to the knees with the mess caused by the high-pressure hoses used to undercut the cover.

"It's fantastic!" she shouted exuberantly as she flung her arms around Ian. "Isn't it fantastic?"

The others were too astonished to do more than nod.

What was being revealed was a low building, consisting of a hexagonal base some twenty metres on a side, of indeterminate height because as yet the digging machines were a long way from the base of its walls. But its height was unimportant. What did matter was that on its roof, glistening in the sunshine and not simply from wet but from the vividness of its colours—blue, red, green, yellow, in alternating hexagons that were large and regular on the back, small and regular around the midsection, much smaller and less distinct but still very regular below . . .

A statue. Unmistakably, a statue of a Draconian. But at least eight times life-size.

"Marvelous!" Rorschach whispered.

"And amazingly close to our reconstructions, too!" Nadine said in high delight. "Apart from size, I mean. Though I never dared guess that they had such beautiful patterns on their skin!"

Proudly leading Ian by the arm, urging him towards the platform level with the statue from which Igor was directing the machines, Cathy said, "We spotted the regular shape of the building, of course, which is why we chose this spot to make a deep trench, but at first we thought the thing on the roof was just a pile of rubble. Goodness knows what it's finished with, but that surface has some very weird electrical properties and gave back the most misleading reflections. But you haven't heard the half of it."

"Very exact," Igor rumbled, wiping sweat from his face with one hand as he carefully re-aimed a water hose by remote control. "You, and we, have seen a quarter. Buried under all this muck, *there* and *there* and *there*"—he pointed at the stratified, sectioned walls of the pit—"there are three other buildings apparently identical with this one, and each would appear to have another similar statue on the roof."

"I can almost imagine," Ian said soberly, "the ghosts of the Draconians chuckling at the way they keep springing surprises on us."

XIII

Mystery piled upon enigma now in a manner unprecedented even on this world full of insoluble riddles. Straightaway Rorschach summed up the situation and gave orders that accorded with Igor's recommendation: for the time being, their full resources must be concentrated on this particular site, while the others could be left to automatic machines and supervised remotely from the base.

He also instructed Karen to prepare the makings of temporary accommodation and ship them here by heavy-duty hovercraft, and rig extra line-of-sight relays to cope with the enormous mass of data bound to be flooding the computers.

Within five days, the base had effectively been transferred to the peat site; only a skeleton staff would henceforth remain at the original location.

And even with all their personnel on hand, they found themselves dazed, baffled, confused, at the plethora of new discoveries.

It was clear that Ian's brilliant notion of making a simulated Draconian was going to have to be postponed indefinitely. But he didn't regret that fact. It had been intended as a way out of a temporary dead end. Now there was the chance that some other, brand-new avenue of attack might offer itself.

Working furiously, but hardly daring to stop even when they neared exhaustion for fear that the machines might uncover some all-important new object when they were asleep, Igor and Cathy and Sue and Olaf and the rest of the archeological team exposed the matching four buildings with painstaking thoroughness. Meantime, Nadine Shah and Lucas Wong studied the statues with the aid of Ruggiero.

There were indeed four of them, one per building, and as nearly as could be defined they were identical, apart from incidental damage during their long period underground. Why, why, *why* should the first-ever naturalistic sculpture found here be on a monumental scale? These statues were without precedent; not even figurines or dolls had been dug up before.

And then came more unanswerable questions.

As the digging machines reached the original ground level, they revealed a surface very like an earthly pavement, cracked and deformed now but obviously once all of one piece, a poured layer as durable as concrete made of grit bonded in a resin chemically akin to epoxy glue. On it were fragments of roughly cobbled, virtually primitive devices: a wheel and a rod that might have been an axle and a bearing or trunnion that didn't fit it properly, suggesting some kind of simple cart; another, detectable chiefly because of the metal cramps which had held it together when most of its substance, perhaps wooden, had rotted to leave only smudges of anomalous compounds in the peat, incontestably—so the computer reconstructions claimed—a cross between a barrow and a sled, a container to be dragged along on a plain runner, without even one wheel. . . .

So out of keeping with the master-craftsmanship of the buildings, let alone the artistic brilliance of those statues!

The entrance to the first building proved to conform to the usual doorless Draconian pattern. Ian and Igor had thrashed out a theory to account for that; suppose, they said, that anything solid enough to be what we would call a door was also solid enough to isolate the occupants from the interplay of electrical fields outside—then it would follow that they'd find the situation intolerable, just as a man shut in a sensory-deprivation tank with neither light nor sound will go insane. Something might once have plugged those openings to conserve heat, but it would have been thin and soft and easily destroyed by time.

Just inside, they made a series of even more astonishing discoveries.

First, they came on a vast printed crystal: ten metres long, al-

most two metres high, emanating—very weakly, but unmistakably
—a single clear pattern of resonance. Then, beyond, they came
into a wide-open hall, lighted by day from above because, as it
turned out, the material from which the statue on the roof was
constructed was translucent, and admitted soft coloured luminance,
much like a stained-glass window.

There were objects, artefacts, blocks of crystal, blocks of some
kind of plastic, countless things distributed randomly around the
floor. But what was most important was that here were also a full
score of Draconian corpses, excellently preserved by comparison
with any that had been studied before, and including for the first
time ever a full range of the species: from a sedentary old female,
perhaps already into the dusk of senility, clear down to a baby, no
longer than a man's forearm.

Lucas and Nadine shouted unashamedly for joy when they came
on this treasure trove, and instantly set about examining them.

Within a day, they were prepared to state categorically that for
the first time the human investigators had tapped into the decadent,
preterminal phase of the natives' existence.

"But how can you be so certain so quickly?" Ruggiero demanded
when they announced their opinions to the assembled company
that night over the evening meal. Here, there was none of the
comparative luxury to be found at the base; they sat on stools and
ate with their plates on their knees, and all that stood between
them and the chill of the night was a two-layer inflatable which
Karen had hastily had made from a simple plastic.

Nobody cared.

"Three main reasons," Nadine said. "First, although the soft internal organs were destroyed very quickly by putrefying bacteria
just as they would have been at home, something stopped the process before the outer integument was seriously affected, and the
actual skeletal structure is virtually intact. We've found what can
only have been congenital deformities. Ankylosed joints, for example, particularly in the case of the baby, which exhibits complete
fusion of one joint in each forelimb and two other fusions in the
walking limbs.

"Second, the associated artefacts. One of them is—was—still clutching what we recognised after a bit of 'that's familiar' as a regular Type H-2 artefact, but carefully ground down to make a knife. Or some sort of cutting tool, anyway."

"Excuse me," Karen said. "For the moment I forget what H-2 is."

"Glass with embedded strands of something apparently organic, about nineteen or twenty centimetres long."

"Oh, yes. Now I know what you mean. You say ground down?"

"No doubt of it. By rubbing on a smooth piece of rock." Nadine stretched and suppressed a yawn. "One can still detect traces of the rock in the parallel microscopic grooves that converge towards the sharp end."

"I find the case convincing already," Rorschach said. "But what's your third point?"

Lucas took up the tale. "Even the skin patterns are preserved," he said. "You must have noticed that when you broke in here, Igor?"—with a glance at the elderly archeologist. "And they're diffuse. Irregular. You might say deformed. While those on the statues are perfectly regular."

"That I'm not convinced by," Igor said. "Why should not they have idealised their monumental statuary? We do."

"Far more important," Olaf Mukerji said, "why *only* monumental statuary?"

"I think I can answer that," Ruggiero said suddenly, and snapped his fingers. "Yes! Ian, you'd be the person to put this idea to, which just this moment hit me. I've been calibrating the properties of the substance those statues are built from, and I can say definitely that it's extremely sophisticated. It doesn't behave the way you'd expect in any band of the spectrum bar visible light. I'm not talking about X rays or gamma rays, obviously. But in terms of—oh—ambient electrical fields, above all, it's doing things I didn't think were possible." He set aside his food plate and hunched forward.

"Could it be that they didn't make statues until they were technologically advanced enough to create a substance that—well, that gave back a signal corresponding to a real Draconian? In other words, until they could make a statue that was lifelike in electrical as well as visual terms?"

"It figures," Ian said at once. "Thank you, Ruggiero; I like it! I'll go see if there's any correspondence between the signal from the giant printed crystal and—"

"Tomorrow!" Rorschach boomed as Ian made to rise and leave. "We still have a year and a half before the ship comes back, you know!"

Ian gave a rueful grin and resumed his seat.

"And there's something I propose to do tomorrow, too," Igor said. They all glanced at him. He went on, "We know the Draconians liked areas of high humidity, as one would expect, moist air being a good conductor and dry air a very poor one. Hence, for instance, their neglect of such areas as the high arid plateau where the base is. But I'm wondering whether there are enough data in store for us to recover something about the meteorological patterns of a hundred thousand years ago. It was what Ruggiero just said that reminded me of this point; it occurred to me a few years ago, and there were insufficient data then, and I'd forgotten again until now. Nadine!"

"Yes?"

"You've mainly concentrated on animal life, I think, but I presume you've studied vegetation, too?"

She hesitated long enough for Lucas to say, "Of course. We had to from the beginning, to make sure what species were best suited for conversion into food and plastics."

"Now, I'm ignorant in this area," Igor said, leaning forward. "But I seem to recall reading that—oh—a forest can change the local climate. Is there any way we can determine whether the Draconians deliberately altered the climate to facilitate their expansion?"

Ian whistled and slapped his knee, and someone behind him clapped hands.

"We should be able to establish that, yes," Lucas said with a pleased smile. "You mean see if the plants associated with city-sites form a continuum?"

"More or less," Igor agreed.

"But in some cases we know they did," Nadine said. "We've been assuming that when a species of plant was taken from one continent to another it was for food. We've found, for example, seeds right at this site here which belong to species widespread only on another continent. And even some fairly well preserved fronds."

"But we haven't specifically checked to see whether any are plants that encourage moisture in the air," Lucas countered. "It's a useful new line of approach, isn't it?"

"Oh yes!" Nadine said, nodding. "We'll certainly programme a computer to follow it up."

After that there was a short pause, broken at last by Rorschach, who gave a chuckle.

"Know something? I like you a lot! I love working with you. Every time we reach a new plateau of discovery, you can be relied on to mull things over for a while and generate a thousand new ideas in quick-fire succession. Lucas, I predict a lot of insomnia tonight. Suppose you ask around and see if anybody wants tranquilizing. Me, I'm tired. I'm going to say good night—and I'll be the first on the list for a tranquilizer, please, because my brain is whirring like a turbine."

Half an hour later, in the companionable darkness of the tent they were sharing now, Ian said sleepily to Cathy, "You know, you're a better tranquilizer than any that comes in a pill."

She gave him a playful jab in the ribs. "So that's what you make love to me for!"

He chuckled and drew her down close to him. Resting his cheek against the softness of her hair, he said, "In a way, yes. That *is* why."

"What? What do you mean?"

"Oh . . ." With the arm he didn't have around her shoulders, he made a gesture in the air. "I guess what I mean is that you've worked a marvelous transformation in me. When I came here, I was scared and worried and—and outright terrified, on a very deep level of my mind. Now I'm not. I get dreadfully frustrated now and then, but because you're you and because you decided you liked me, I'm able to digest it and recover and carry on." He hesitated. "What I really mean, I suspect, is that I love you very much."

There was a moment of silence. Then, in a changed voice, Cathy said, "I'm beginning to love you, too, Ian. In a way I never felt for anyone before except Dugal. A closeness. A sense of intimacy.

'Bone of my bone, flesh of my flesh . . .' Except that it's more 'mind of my mind,' if you follow me."

"That's right," Ian said, and hugged her tightly.

Nothing else, for the time being, seemed worth saying, and Ian was almost sure Cathy had dozed off when suddenly she said, "Do you suppose the Draconians fell in love?"

"I don't know," Ian said in surprise. "Maybe. . . . No! No, I doubt it, on reflection. If it's true they constantly communicated one with another just by existing, then very probably they'd have been in much the same relationship as a brother and sister, as it were—except, since all females were elderly, it might have been more parental. You loved Dugal, but you never fell in love with him."

"I see what you mean," she murmured. "The same thing used to happen in a kibbutz, didn't it? At least according to some authorities."

"Right; I ran across that, too. Kids raised in close association, much like members of one large family, tended to be reflexively exogamous. They married out of the community more often than they married within it. And if it's really true that the Draconians expanded smoothly from one focal point, then they would all have belonged to one community, as it were, and the situation would scarcely have been conducive to what we call falling in love."

"Poor things," Cathy said drowsily. "What they missed . . . !"

And, a minute later, she was fast asleep.

XIV

Little by little, the same process as usual overtook all the new discoveries: they erupted like lava from the crater of a volcano, and glowed and flowed for a while—longer than at any other stage since humans arrived here, granted, but doomed to the same fate in the end—and finally they cooled into the dull, grey, obdurate mass of another insoluble problem.

It took almost half a year for that stage to be reached, however. Nearly to the midpoint of his first tour here, Ian was kept abuzz with the continual stimulus of fresh suggestions.

In the other three identical buildings, there were no well-preserved corpses, but there were skeletal remains, and in nearby buildings others were found, many of them being somewhat deformed, too. Moreover they kept unearthing more primitive constructs and tools, right on the topmost layer above the pavement, as they moved outward from the centre. It was generally agreed within a couple of months that this could well have been the spot where the last of the race came to huddle and wait for death. Another indication that this was a safe assumption was presented when a skeleton of an old female was found with a hideously deformed embryo's skeleton enclosed in the womb area; no trace of the hide or internal organs had survived, and a predator or carrion-eater had gnawed the bones, but enough remained in association with each other for the situation to be reconstructed by the computers.

"Is it possible," Rorschach asked Igor and Ian, "that they regarded those statues as some sort of magic charm? Were they dying out because of some dominant harmful mutation, and did they erect the statues as a last desperate appeal to the powers that be? Something idealised, beautiful, glamorous in the strict sense . . . ?"

Ian clawed his beard. "It's a sound speculation," he admitted. "But somehow it doesn't jibe with the impression of the natives' psychology that I'm evolving in my mind."

Igor glanced at him sharply. "Why not? Look, we've established that those huge printed crystals, one at the entrance of each of the four buildings—go ahead and call them temples, I'd say!—each of the four resonates a single loud pattern. To the Draconians they must have been as deafening as a siren!"

"True enough, and the pattern is very simple and very clear," Ian conceded. "But the whole sequence of their development runs counter to the idea. They seem to have hit on a grand plan, and stuck to it for about three millennia, and collapsed so abruptly that they were back to the simplest and most primitive devices in the blink of an eye. Now, I simply can't make myself believe that if they'd been handicapped by belief in capricious supernatural beings they'd have achieved what they did. And for the notion of gods or fate or what-have-you to appear at the very last moment . . . No, it rings false."

"Unless they did have religious convictions right back at the beginning, discarded them and retained only the memory of their existence as a historical curiosity," Rorschach offered. "That might explain why they reappeared at the eleventh hour."

"Ye-es. . . ." But Ian still sounded doubtful. "I'll add it to my computerised hypotheses, see if the machines can come up with any pointers to it. But I can't in good faith assign it a high priority."

"I'm not asking you to," Rorschach murmured. "It's just that for the first time since we discovered Ash I have time on my hands. Everyone is so busy, they aren't creating administrative problems."

"Just as well," Igor grunted. "Problems of our own would be superfluous, given the quantity we've had wished on us by the natives."

Occasional breakthroughs continued. It was with high delight that Nadine came to report spin-off from Igor's remark about plants that would tend to keep the local humidity high.

"We ran a complete review of all our data about the vegetation," she announced. "Not only does your idea check out, Igor, because we've discovered something that's been right under our noses and should have been spotted long ago, but we got a bonus with it."

She had come upon them while they were impatiently waiting for the digging machines to remove another metre-thick layer of the cover; at this depth, the decayed vegetable matter was so compressed that it was lignitic, on the way to becoming coal, and the task was proceeding slowly.

"Well, tell us all about it," Igor invited, leaning back against the rail of the catwalk spanning the now enormous pit.

"First off, we discovered that there was a genetic explosion among the plant life here just about a hundred thousand years ago." Nadine paused impressively.

"Do you mean," Cathy ventured, "that some common cause led to the plants and the animal life mutating?"

"No, that's too wild a guess. What it does look like is proof that the Draconians practised selective breeding of crops. It was to be expected, given their use of bioelectronics, but for some idiotic reason we never actually sought out the evidence before. Igor, we're obliged to you."

Igor waved the compliment aside. Ian said, "You're talking about —oh—the kind of process which evolved wheat from wild grass?"

"Exactly. But not just that. Let me get on to the bonus. It's far more than just proof of something we should have thought of before. Enough unaltered substance remained in the corpses we found over there"—Nadine gestured towards the first of the four identical buildings, now referred to as "temples" despite Ian's misgivings on the matter—"for us to conduct some comparative studies on the germ plasm of the Draconians, and that of the contemporary fauna. Care to guess what we came up with?"

The others exchanged blank looks. Ian suggested, "Proof of selective breeding among animals, too? But surely you'd expect that. We know the Draconians were primarily herbivorous, don't we? But that needn't have prevented them from breeding pets or the counterpart of milch cows!"

"Yes, we did find evidence of that, naturally!" Nadine brushed the point aside impatiently. "But we finally know that they deliberately tailored both plants and animals for use as tools!"

Stunned silence greeted the claim. Eventually Ian said faintly, "How the *hell* . . . ?"

"It's very technical, I'm afraid," Nadine admitted. "I left Lucas trying to figure out how it can be made clear to a nonspecialist because I wanted Igor to be the first to hear about the discovery. Basically, though, what it amounts to is that in several species, both animal and vegetable, we've found organs that appear to have little or no evolutionary purpose. You know we have automatic samplers drifting with the ocean currents all the time, studying aquatic life, and we've been collecting data on land long enough now to have a very good idea of the evolutionary chain here: sometimes amazingly like ours, sometimes taking an unexpected detour, sometimes seeming to jump a stage which on Earth gave rise to a whole complex of life forms. Well, it occurred to me"—Nadine gave a modest cough—"to check whether these anomalous extra organs, which don't appear in the more primitive forms even in embryo, as it were, might be sensitive to electrical fields. They are, all right. We have a whole assortment of different plants in the lab right now, and Lucas is playing field patterns at them, derived from those printed on your crystals, Ian, and they're reacting."

"Hey!" Ian said. "I'm going there right this minute! You two tell me if you find anything equally important—cancel that! Ten times as important!"

"Yes," Lucas said in a didactic tone, "Nadine's right. It looks as though these plants here may be descendants of the earliest counterpart to the bioelectronic system we found on the moon."

He pointed at the array on the lab bench at the end of the room. The plants, in ordinary plastic pots, were an unremarkable selection of commonplace-enough species, but two automatic electronic devices were sliding along a rail above them, somewhat as though the recording and replay heads of a tape recorder were to be moving while the tape remained still. A computer display on another wall made it clear at a glance what was happening. The first of the devices "played" an electrical field over the plants, in a pattern derived from randomly chosen printed crystals; the second, following about a minute later, detected that the field had been impressed on the plants and was resonating in the mysterious organs unrelated to evolutionary need which Nadine had spoken of.

"Very interesting," Ian said thoughtfully, and made to take a closer look. Lucas checked him.

"No, keep away, please. You can't see it from here, but there's a fine mist of water playing all over the bench—a sort of miniature fog—to improve conduction, and I don't want a two-metre pillar of water to cause disturbances in the field!"

Ian chuckled. After a pause, he said, "Tell me, have you thought of any use these plants could have been put to?"

"Be reasonable," Lucas countered. "We only just discovered that the phenomenon exists; it's far too soon to start guessing why."

"I was just wondering about the wall niches we keep finding in all the cities here," Ian murmured. "Every last one, I believe, contains some organic trace. Could these plants have anything to do with that?"

Lucas pursed his lips. "That's a very sensible suggestion," he said. "Nadine dear, would you—?"

But she was already punching the nearest computer read-in.

Two minutes, and she reported, "We'd have to let a few sample plants rot, or bake them in an oven or something, to simulate a decay process, but if you asked me to give an advance opinion, I'd say yes. Plants like these could very well have been placed in those niches."

"Hmm!" Lucas regarded Ian with respect. "I've been told over and over that you have amazing insights now and then, but this is the first time you've favoured me with the benefit of your talents. I'm impressed. Tell me more. What purpose could they have served?"

Ian spread his hands, blushing vivid red . . . much against his will, but it seemed to be a reflex he was doomed to endure until the end of his days.

"I can think of myriads of possibilities. As to the interior ones . . . Well, how about amplification of natural signals? They could well have needed a communication or data processing system, the way we use phones and so forth. As to the outdoor ones, they could be anything from weather detectors to—to route indicators, signposts for people wanting to visit another city! Or they could identify an address, or they could relay news of public importance, or they could—" He broke off, grinning. "*You* go on!"

Lucas gave an answering chuckle. "Yes, I take the point. Talk about being premature. . . . Still, we now have something really concrete to work on. It would be even better if you were to crack the language for us, though." He gave Ian a keen glance. "Making any progress in that area?"

"I'm afraid not. I've turned most of it over to the machines, you know. Sifting the well-printed crystals for the sort of patterns that might give us a clue because they recur in identical contexts would be difficult enough for a team of a hundred experts; for me, virtually single-handed, it's ridiculous. But there is one thing that's becoming alarmingly clear." He scowled, looking into nowhere.

"What?" Nadine demanded, coming to stand at his side.

"There's the most amazing degree of resemblance from one crystal to another. I mean, almost to the point where you could believe they were originally identical and have just been altered by the passage of time."

"But I thought—" Lucas began, and checked, biting his lip.

"You thought they varied tremendously one from another? So did I!" Ian sounded rueful. "Unfortunately it turns out that much of the contrast from one to the next is due—or at any rate ascribable —to the in-built piezo effect, which you know about, I think."

They both nodded.

"Constant pressure, from varying weights of overlay, has super-posed an irrelevant signal on each crystal. Now that I've managed to programme the computers to eliminate this chance effect, every approximation brings me closer to an underlying identity. It's infuriating! But it does prove one thing: We don't have to do with anything like a book or a recording of music. What we actually do have, though . . . Any ideas? It would be a fair trade if you gave me an insight, too, hm?"

Lucas and Nadine stared at each other. Eventually Nadine said,

"But if they were originally identical, why have so many of them?"

"You tell me!"

Lucas shook his head. "No, I have no ideas at all. All I can think of at the moment is my own problem."

"I thought you'd just solved one," Ian said with a smile.

"Which, as usual, has dragged another in by the tail." Lucas leaned back against the edge of the nearest bench, his plump haunches deforming against the hard square metal.

"Right now the likeliest theory we have about the fate of the aliens is that they were overtaken by a deleterious mutation. Correct?"

"It's the leader by a mile," Ian grunted.

"In that case, given what we've just demonstrated about their knowledge of genetics—their ability to modify plants and probably animals to use as scientific instruments—how in the whole wide galaxy could they have overlooked and failed to cope with a mutation in their own germ plasm that was obviously apt to exterminate them?"

Lucas shook his head with an expression of pure incredulity.

"It makes absolutely no sense to me. Not a sliver! Not a smidgen!"

The lava of hot new ideas solidified into a grey dull mass just about at the same time as the rainy season arrived, and a huge gloomy inflatable dome had to be erected over the peat site. The drumming of the continual downpour, which would last for at least forty and probably more like fifty days, was no more welcome for being inevitable; it seemed like a ruffle of funeral drums.

Rorschach therefore decreed that it was time to return to main base and hold the monthly review conference there, in the hot sunlight which all of them had so often complained about, but which at least did not possess the mind-dulling quality of this steady monotonous downpour.

His judgment, as usual, was accurate. When the first session of the conference assembled, people were already looking a lot happier, thanks to luxuries that were not available at the temporary base on the mainland, such as sonic cleansing machines for their clothes—they had been doing their laundry the ancient way, with water and detergents—beds that were better than sticky inflatable oblong cushions and a far wider choice of diet than the portable food converters could supply.

Heard in this context, so comfortingly redolent of faraway Earth, the summary initial accounts of progress from each successive department seemed more impressive. It was as though, out at the peat site, one felt dominated by the past. Here there was the chance to rediscover a belief in the future.

Ian pondered that until the time came for him to give his own report, and then repeated more or less what he had already told

Nadine and Lucas. It did not sound much better than before; still, he could comfort himself with the argument that even negative knowledge was useful.

When everybody had concluded what they had to say, Rorschach took a sip of the beer he had before him in a stein which Karen, on the spur of the moment, had had made for him on discovering that this conference coincided with his fifty-fifth birthday, and said musingly, "One thing strikes me, listening to you all."

They looked expectant.

"You seem to be talking as though you've reached a dead end in every last area. I'm puzzled. To me, it sounds more as though you're making constant breakthroughs."

"Valentine?" Igor said, gesturing.

"Yes?"

"You're nearly right in what you say." The elderly chief archeologist hunched forward, cupping a glass of wine between his hands. "Naturally, as a result of discovering our very splendid identical buildings—out of deference to Ian, I won't call them temples!—as a result of that, we have indeed made a hell of a lot of progress. *But . . . !*"

He sipped his wine before resuming.

"*But,*" he said again, more forcefully still, "we're caught in a vicious-circle process. True, we know far more about the natives than we expected to half a year ago; we've been amazingly lucky, which is another way of saying we've kept our eyes and minds open and responded when something turned up. On the other hand, though, precisely because we have collected so many new facts, we have many, many more combinations we can make of them. Each of us, in our own way, could be regarded as having the same problem that Ian does: so long as we are simply gathering data, without a tentative framework to hang them on, we're going to go on being frustrated more than we're pleased. I therefore wish to move that we revive Ian's plan to build a simulated Draconian and see if we can develop a strong hypothesis, on the basis of his recommendations, against which to test what we think we know."

"Seconded!" Cathy said promptly from her place at Ian's side.

"Before I invite the meeting to discuss the motion," Rorschach said, "what does Ian think?"

Ian pondered a long moment before replying. He said, "I'm willing, if people don't think it would take up too much time and distract us from work at Peat."

Ruggiero raised his hand. "I don't see how it could," he said. "Igor's right: simply making a grand pile of data is ridiculous. By now we ought to have enough to start fitting them together. Ian's approach to that seems to be the only valid one so far put forward."

"Does anybody disagree violently?" Rorschach inquired, and when nobody else spoke up continued, "So resolved, then. Achmed, Karen, would you two make yourselves responsible for finding out what's been worked out by the programme we left running to design a simulated native, and report back tomorrow? We can constitute ourselves a ways and means committee and start estimating how long the project will take. Ian, how long do you reckon on spending—uh—in disguise?"

Ian shrugged. "Certainly a month or two, possibly more. But if any of us has reached a genuine dead end, it has to be me; I literally have no ideas at all of where I can go from here. The more I study the printed crystals, the more certain I become that if they were not absolutely identical, they may have differed in such subtle ways that time has wiped out the crucial information. So I'd better simply say: as long as necessary."

"Beg to differ," Lucas said mildly. "You're not going to cut yourself off from us indefinitely. Sorry. I simply won't permit it. You'll be monitored constantly, and medically examined at regular and frequent intervals. Say, at least every month. And you'll signal daily from wherever you are. By the way, where would you go? Obviously there's too much happening at Peat."

"Yes, of course," Ian said. "I was going to pick Ash. It's nearly as well preserved, and it's been a long time since anything unique turned up there, so withdrawing the machines for a while wouldn't cause any real problems. Yes, I'd say Ash."

"I think we should consider building two simulacra," Cathy said. "Ian, wouldn't it make things easier? I mean, if these people interacted constantly, being alone—"

"With you inside the other one, you mean?" Ian interrupted. He shook his head, smiling. "Sorry, no. If the trick can be worked—which I'm not promising—I'll have to do it by myself. Having another mock native around who was thinking human would be less than helpful . . . particularly if you were my partner. It could cause all sorts of—uh—distractions!"

"Pity," Cathy said, leaning back. "But I take the point."

When everybody was called to the important new discovery at Peat, a programme had been left on standby status in the base computers, instructed to compile all relevant data including new additions and develop a design for the simulacrum. By now it had incorporated information based on the four statues, and when they tapped into the result, they found the design complete except for a couple of finishing touches. Inevitably it was in the male phase; computer reconstruction of the elderly female found recently had shown what Nadine had long suspected, that when fertilised and gravid the natives became virtually sessile, capable of moving only short distances, if at all, without assistance. Many of the contemporary fauna followed the same pattern, so it was scarcely surprising.

There were all kinds of interesting implications in that which Ian planned to think through when he launched out on his lonely adventure into the mind of another—long extinct—race.

Gradually the simulacrum started to take shape; first they constructed the skeleton with its cleverly articulated joints and then they inserted within it a cradle to support Ian and a miniaturised power pack capable of driving it indefinitely provided it received at least four hours of bright sunlight per day. This was nothing Ian could help with, except to go and "try it on" occasionally like a suit of clothes. He spent most of his time for the next several weeks being repeatedly hypnotised by Lucas, first with the help of a drug, then without. He proved to be an apt subject.

Then came the question of the machine-man interface. It was very difficult to devise means of making Ian feel the motion of six limbs instead of four, but Nadine suggested a solution. Evolution-

arily speaking, the manipulating appendages of the natives weren't
legs at all, but more akin to lips, changed in much the same way as
an elephant's nose changed into a trunk. She suggested making the
grasping limbs mechanical, but with direct connections to Ian's
face and chin, a proposal that Ian promptly approved.

That left him with the four legs reporting as though he were
quadrupedal, but not moving, and that gave Lucas headaches. He
was much worried by the risk entailed in having Ian's real limbs
motionless for so long; he talked about cramp, chafing, atrophy.
There were cures for all, but fitting them into so narrow a compass
was another matter.

It was Ian himself who suggested that into the sensors which
were going to be attached to his skin and report heat and cold and
other tactile data they should incorporate tiny stimulators based on
those used to maintain muscle tone in people temporarily paralysed.
Tests showed that that was feasible. Good tone was maintained
during a forty-eight-hour test, and circulation remained excellent.
He emerged a trifle stiff, but pronounced himself otherwise very
satisfied.

Next they solved the problem of making him react to external
electrical fields in as nearly as possible the same way as a native
animal. Ruggiero spent a long time on that and triumphantly produced a marvel of lightweight engineering: sensors and generators
—to bathe Ian in his own field and make him aware of it much as
one is aware of a nose, visible but ignored—were combined into tiny
flat pads that would rest on his bare skin and signal ambient currents in the form of pressure.

Rorschach's hasty idea of making use of the magnetic response
of the retina was ruled out as potentially very dangerous, but since
the discovery of the four statues it had become clear that the natives
had had a keen colour sense and no doubt regarded it as important,
perhaps in a manner parallel to the way humans regard pitch and
timbre: not the most, but the next-most, important means of garnering information about the world around.

Each time Ian put on the simulacrum, he reported to Lucas how
well he was responding to the sensory inputs, and Lucas selected
what aspects he could reinforce by hypnosis. In an astonishingly

short time, less than three months, Ian was beginning to dream in a mode he had never experienced before. On waking, he recalled not visual images, but patterns of swirling warmth, cold, pressure, near pain—not actual pain, just a sensation that was very, very disturbing.

And very exciting, too.

On the night before the simulacrum was due to be put to the ultimate test, a full-scale month-long trial at the Ash site, Cathy said wistfully into the darkness of the room they now shared, "I do wish you could make me understand how it feels, Ian. I'm getting quite envious of you."

"If I could tell you, I would," he answered soberly. "And in a little while, I expect I shall be able to. Already I can draw analogies."

"For example . . . ?"

He hesitated, then gave an unexpected chuckle. "I don't know whether what I have in mind works for women as well as men—and doesn't it make my project seem ludicrous, when I'm setting out to think like a Draconian and I don't even know something quite commonplace about the other sex of my own species?"

"Stop beating about the bush, will you?" She pinched his arm.

"Would you believe that pinch feels solid, but magnetically permeable, and about eighty kilograms in mass ten centimetres away?"

She whistled softly. "Ay-ay-ay! You mean that literally? That's the way it really feels to you?"

"Yes, even without being put into trance."

She hesitated awhile, and eventually said, "I was talking about you to Karen the other day. Is it true that when you first met her you said your brain was like a haunted house?"

"Yes. Not in any frightening way," he hastened to add. "More . . . more it's that I sense overtones. Echoes. Implications." He waved vaguely to embrace a world of possibilities. "But I never dreamed I'd make so many cross-associations from one sense to another as I can with the mock Draconian."

"I believe you," she muttered. "What was the thing you said you don't know about women?"

"Oh!" He laughed aloud this time. "Well, when you have to wait a long time before relieving yourself, do you get a sort of upside-down pain when you finally let go?"

"Yes!" She started upright on the bed. "I know just what you mean! 'Upside-down pain'—I never thought of expressing it like that, but it's exact! Know something?"

"Mm-hm?"

"If you can capture a sensation that vividly in a neat new phrase . . ." She lay down again, seeming thoughtful. "I guess I don't have to be worried about what's been bothering me. Maybe it's doing you an injustice—in fact, now I'm sure it is—but I have been wondering how you'd explain to the rest of us what came of your experiment if you honestly did start to think in Draconian patterns. I see how, now you've given me an example. I'm glad. It's taken a weight off my mind."

"That kind of 'upside-down pain,'" Ian said, "indicates a tremendous mass with very low magnetism all around, like a big building. I had it very intensely in the refectory. . . . Hell, what am I doing rambling on at such length? I ought to be doing something entirely different that I may not have the chance to do again for months!"

He rolled over towards her. Some time later she said, close to his ear, "At least I can be sure of one thing. No matter how efficient the simulacrum is, you're not going to leave me for some dowager Draconian, are you? Still, you might see if they could have offered humans any hints!"

XVI

He woke into a different universe.

For a while he waited, digesting the impact of his surroundings at the site named Ash—

It doesn't have that name. It has no name. Moreover I am not called Ian Macauley. I am "I," but in a sense less than that. Others flow and interact even though they are not here.

He wrenched his mind away from contemplation of things that related to being human (though a Draconian had no knowledge of other intelligence *a priori*, so would think a concept meaning human, of my own kind) and spent many minutes exploring his surroundings without moving. It was almost dark in this place; nonetheless, he knew exactly what there was here. With sudden surprise he realised that the walls and floor tingled, though the ceiling/roof did not.

Hmm! Why . . . ? Ah: iron traces in the material used to build it.

He carefully avoided thinking: *that they built it with.* The whole goal and purpose of this test was to strip away every element of his thinking that related to a species which would not visit this planet for another thousand centuries.

When he was satisfied that, despite the low light level, he knew to within a centimetre or so where the walls and the entrance were, he shut his eyes and found his way to the latter by nontouch, by the little tickles and light sensations of pressure which were fed into his skin and thence to his nerves by the miniaturised transducers in his . . . *body.*

His practice at the base stood him in good stead. He was over-large compared to the vanished inhabitants of this city, but he steered a precise course through the doorway, then along a passage, and then into the open air, where he halted to conduct another review of his surroundings. He did not bump or scrape the walls, even with eyes closed.

This was his talent, the thing he could do better, perhaps, than any living man: learn another mode of thought. But until now those other modes had always been, at bottom, human and consequently not very far removed from his ordinary processes of mentation. They might swarm with godlings and evil spirits and mistaken notions of the nature of the air and the land and the oceans, but they could be reached by merely peeling away modern sophistication and substituting artificial naïveté. Hands remained, eyes, belly, gonads.

Now it was necessary for those to be shed, too, and in their place would have to come alien senses, alien likes and dislikes, alien imaginings. Perhaps it was impossible.

Still, it was starting well.

He had emerged from a small building, purpose unknown, at the western side of a large open space: a market, perhaps, because charred vegetable remains had been found under the layer of volcanic debris. One could hazard a guess at some kind of display table, fixed or mobile, on which were arrayed plants . . . for sale?

Good question. What did these people do to organise their trade? Did they trade? It seems very probable. Here in the centre of a great city, with its pavements of grit-in-glue, there would have had to be food. They ate vegetables. No plants in quantities large enough to provide nourishment for a million-strong population could be grown within kilometres of here—

He checked that thought, too. A kilometre was a meaningless measure now. Strike that and replace it with "as long a distance as I could walk in a quarter of a day" or something of the sort.

His eyes were still shut, but he could discern the change from interior to exterior very clearly. Overhead, a vast nothing; underfoot, another tingling surface, but different in character from what he had awoken to. (Yes, the Draconians would have slept; he'd made sure about that, confirming that contemporary animals did so. Lucas had lectured him exhaustively on the inevitable incidence of sleep among creatures with highly organised nervous systems. . . . *Stop! No such person as Lucas!*)

Close at his back, the wall of the building he had left with the doorway gap in it; to right, left, and in front, other walls, also with gaps where streets/alleys ran (and he consciously imposed aware-ness of four walking limbs, not two, on that metaphorical "ran"), casting back at him a sort of radar echo . . . except it was not a pulse-emitted-echo-received sensation, it was a there-it-is sensation, perfectly continuous.

He thought in delight: *Oh, they've done a fantastic job for me!*

And cancelled that along with every subsequent recollection of humanity.

Next, then, a fleeting problem.

Whom do I thank for having been created as myself?

Too early to start investigating the subtlest, least conscious as-pects. Too early to wonder about parental-filial relationships. Suf-ficient for the moment to try to picture in imagination the busy-ness of this(?) market.

People. Instead of a clear signal of that distant wall, a multiple hum of pressure (as it were) moving and intertwining . . . good, yes, must have been a bit like that. (A flicker in his mind, based on the tingling of his skin, making a pattern that hinted at compre-hensibility.) Some reference to hunger, perhaps? If food stuffs were(?) sold here, did I come out to break my night's fast?

File that as entirely possible but unconfirmed!

Now, having completed his imaginary picture, he opened his eyes and saw the present reality: a greyish-white expanse of hard ground, blank to the new daylight.

Vacancy.

Yet not still, not inactive. Hereabouts, at this season, the weather was clement: humidity high, conductivity excellent. No electrical tension in the low overcast. In a word—fine.

He began to move, and at random made for a southerly exit from the open space. In a little while he realised he was going downhill, towards a level where excavation had revealed the bed of a former river. The Draconians had liked to have a river running through their cities. Unsurprisingly. As he went, he pictured(?) modified plants in wall niches, signalling to him: directions? News? Knowledge of some sort, very likely.

But now the river was dry. Its course had been remade by the volcano's lava—*stop! Not for centuries yet! It is a river for me, it's water, I'm getting the right impulses because I'm sure, absolutely sure, I'd head for a damp area if I had no obligation to do otherwise.*

Following which, a question which later grew to be crucial: *When would I have no obligation to do otherwise . . . ?*

That too, though, was excessively subtle to be considered this early in the project.

The days passed, and by gradual stages his conception of life as a Draconian rounded out, took on detail, became colourful. He grew able to discard words from his thinking and replace them with "equates-to-tingle-pattern" . . . but he was mostly unaware that that was happening, except during the one hour each evening when, under posthypnotic compulsion, he returned to his "home" and ate human food and used a human-built device to report that he was well and happy.

He did not talk, even then. He simply pressed a button that activated remote sensors in his body, and a cross section of their impulses was flashed to a satellite and thence to the main base.

The chief question after the first ten days or so was a simple but incredibly difficult one: *What do I do?*

Initially he was quite content to accept that Draconians thought, reflected, considered, invented, more than (suppress this) human beings. Would perhaps take a long while over a private plan, then implement it and see it succeed first time.

But additional insights conglomerated into a whole, and new ideas were spawned. . . .

Spawned?

In all the places where, obviously, there had been great activity (market?, laboratory?, library?, ******?), he kept recalling that there was active-male, passive-female, and . . .

(Now he was losing words more and more; the transition to symbols that weren't symbols, but called up to consciousness real-time physical sensations, was gathering momentum, and the experience was giddying but vastly exciting.)

And I'm going to make the change myself.

Friends? Yes, of course—that is, persons whose patterns strike a chord of recognition. Fifteen days, nearly twenty (but I count, most likely, to a base two, I suspect), and I never spoke to anybody, never interacted!

A night of dreams of horrible, fearful, unspeakable loneliness— *Click.*

I know who I am. Suddenly I'm quite sure who I am. I'm neuter. No wonder my friends won't talk to me right now.

I've lived the active part of my life. What I was able to do, with complete mobility, is done. I am growing slower and more awkward in my movements (I feel I move awkwardly, there are deep aches, deep as my bones, penetrating me like blades) in spite of . . .

Did I try to stave it off? Yes, I think so. There is advanced modern medicine, practised solely by my friends the active males. In olden times it was taken for granted, the changeover; now, nothing is taken for granted at all—we fly, we shoot to the moon, we work miracles, thought out beforehand.

Yet and still, there is an eventual limit. With what to be looked forward to?

He puzzled that, pondered it, grew so frustrated he wanted to weep . . . except that that wasn't right. Tears-eyes: of secondary importance. Instead, a discernible change in the body field. Causing others to shy away! Yes, yes! *Anger!*

But, again: what to look forward to? Surely something, some compensation, some consolation (what was that? Compensation . . . ? Like an itch in the brain, can't be scratched but one desperately wants to!).

It had turned out that the use of the pronoun "one" instead of "I" was infinitely more apt.

As though resigned already to completing his life in a stiff sessile mode, he spent long hours at the side of the dry empty river, among no-longer-existent plants that clung to its muddy banks, feeling the soothing caress of the current by force of will, groping, creeping, striving towards acceptance of senility . . . but not that yet. Between now and then some climax, some repayment for the sacrifice of activity, some reward, some—something.

He often felt giddy, disoriented, at a loss. Until it was treated, he had suffered migraine during childhood, and knew the obsessive-compulsive repetition of a single random phrase which typically associated to the onset of his aura. Now he was being infuriated by concepts revolving around a centre: reward for, compensation for, reimbursement for, just fee for, look back on and feel satisfied (in a crazy confusion, a garbled blend of apprehension and assurance)—

Insurance?

Frustrated not because of the change of life which is the fate of us all, but because somehow I didn't—make provision properly?

?

It eluded him, like a darting fish, like the rainbow's end (pot of gold but makes no sense, I know what a pot is but gold is for use, it's a superb conductor and I don't care that it's yellow because more importantly I feel its nature) or like those ballonet-borne treetop-sleeping creatures that soar landwards on the morning breeze, seawards again after sunset.

Frustration stretched out over days and days turned easily to thoughts of: competition, being done down, being outmanoeuvred . . . but just a second, we don't do that, do we?

Do we?

Once again, painfully and slowly from the top: We begin as babies, we grow to functional active males, we undergo a neuter transition lasting about a year, we spend a much shorter time as fertile females, we lapse into ultimate senility and—

GOT IT!

But there were strange hideous creatures before him, and he cowered in terror. Things like plants, moving: vertical things, horrible, with too few limbs, impossibly balanced on stalks that planted and rooted and planted and brought them swiftly towards him even though he tried to flee. They caught up, they surrounded him, they uttered some kind of atmospheric vibration that meant nothing and—

It was the infirmary at the base, and Cathy was there at the side of this—this bed he was stretched out in, and by the door (how odd to block an entrance like that, with a solid object!) Lucas Wong, and also present, Rorschach.

"He's waking up!" Cathy exclaimed.

And before the others had a chance to do more than react, he cried out, "Why did you stop me? I was so close—I was so *close!*"

"What you were close to," Lucas said, "was death."

"But I— What?" The word struck through the artificial garb in which he had dressed his mind.

"You nearly died," Lucas emphasised. "You caught a local disease, one of the rare ones that can infect human tissue. When we came to rescue you, you were running four degrees of fever and you hadn't eaten more than a mouthful in three days. You were delirious. You've been lying here unconscious for nearly a week."

"But I was so close!" Ian repeated piteously. "It was all starting to come clear. You've got to let me go back, right away."

"No," Rorschach said, taking a pace towards the bed. "And that's final. It's too dangerous, Ian. What good would it be if you went the same way as the natives?"

"But it wasn't disease!" he exclaimed. "It was . . . It was . . ."

And found he could no more remember the truth he'd stumbled on than a vague and shadowy dream.

XVII

It was very quiet in the base's medical-inspection room. Elsewhere on the planet there were creatures that buzzed and crawled and stridulated after the fashion of earthly insects, but on the high desert plateau there were none to speak of.

Sunlight slanted stark through the big windows, gleaming on sterile metal shelves and furniture, but the chair where Ian sat was in shadow. Before him Lucas Wong, on a high stool, leaned intently forward, while a short distance away in another chair Valentine Rorschach waited impatiently for the result of this experiment.

"If it's true"—so Lucas had argued—"that Ian really was on the verge of a breakthrough when we had to rescue him, then it must have been something he figured out while he was under hypnosis. Among the tricks you can play with that technique is artificial enhancement of the memory. When Ian is better, we'll simply put him back in trance and interrogate him."

And today was the day to try it out.

Rorschach watched with curiosity as Lucas passed his hand once, twice, a third time over Ian's open eyes, fixed on a bright reflection from a mirror angled to beam at the opposite wall. When this was being done in preparation for Ian's month at the Ash site, he himself had been too busy tying together the complicated strands of the simulacrum-building project to come and watch. But right now everything was, if not at a standstill, then at any rate proceeding with a sort of leisurely slackness, as though over the months since Ian's arrival people had grown overused to leaning on him as a source of bright new suggestions, and were marking time in the expectation that he would indeed reveal the answer to the mystery of the natives.

He was worried.

"Your eyelids are growing heavy," Lucas murmured. "You feel sleepy, so-o-o sleepy. . . . When I count to three, you will relax completely, you will close your eyes, you will drift away, you will hear nothing but my voice. . . ."

He droned on soporifically. Rorschach's mind wandered again, recalling how eager Ian had been throughout his period of convalescence, how frustrated he had seemed—clear to the point of breaking out in fits of blind rage—at not being able to recapture the dazzling insight he claimed he had achieved.

For a week or more he had been insisting he was well enough to stand the strain, and Lucas had contradicted him with the evidence of his medical computers to back him up.

Rorschach himself was nearly as excited. He kept rehearing the comment Rudolf Weil had made, and he had always respected Weil's judgment. This, the colonel had said, was the person he would bet on to decipher the native language.

In so short a time . . . ?

But it wasn't so short, not really. Back on Earth Ian had studied every available printed crystal, every snippet of data the *Stellaris* had carried home, had indeed set to work before Igor filed a special request for him to be sent to Sigma Draconis. A man with such an unusual mind, capable of generating patterns where most people would see a jumble of unconnected nonsense—yes, it was entirely possible he had made the breakthrough.

Hurry up, Lucas! For pity's sake get a move on!

He only thought that, though. He was afraid to say it for fear of disturbing the process of induction.

"Okay," Lucas said at last, and wiped a trace of sweat from his forehead with his sleeve. "He's in deep trance again now. Funny, it took longer than it usually does, and that's a bad sign."

"Why?"

"Oh . . ." A vague gesture. "It could imply that what he consciously wants to remember actually proved to be very painful and is being suppressed. Or it could mean, equally, that on the subconscious level he's aware that what he mistook for a brilliant inspiration was nothing of the kind, but a delusion caused by the high fever he was suffering. Ever have a dream in which you were sure you'd hit on a marvelous new idea, and then realised on waking that it was completely ridiculous?"

Rorschach nodded soberly. "I get you. But don't make too many dismal forecasts, please. You could be wrong."

"Sure. Shall we find out?"

"Yes, go ahead!"

Lucas turned back to Ian.

"Ian, can you hear me?"

"I hear you fine." Faintly, his voice seeming to come from a long way off. His lips barely moved.

"Ian, think back now, think back, to the time just before we came to bring you away from Ash. Are you thinking back? Remember it was the time when you were being a Draconian, you'd lived in the native city for a month, you were in a body with four legs and you felt the changing fields all around you. . . . Are you remembering, Ian?"

"Yes, I'm remembering."

"Tell us all about what it felt like to be there, to be in a body with four legs and pick things up with your long hard lips and sense all the pressures and textures of the walls and the land and the currents of the air." Lucas's tone never wavered; he maintained the same soothing pitch and almost inflectionless delivery as he had used when performing the induction.

"It was . . . different."

"How was it different?"

Rorschach stifled a sigh and composed himself more comfortably on his chair. This was going to take a long time.

Little by little they teased out of Ian's memory tantalising hints, and a microphone dutifully recorded every word for later computer study. They heard how he laboriously worked his way from superficial questions—did they trade? Yes, or they would not have been able to feed themselves in the middle of a city; at least they must have used a division of labour—to others, infinitely more subtle, that would barely adapt to human language.

At one point Rorschach could restrain himself no longer. He muttered, "But this is incredible! He really does seem to have got under the natives' skin!"

Pale, Lucas said, "I'm more convinced by the moment. But it would be best if you kept completely quiet."

So onward, through the superficial layers of sexuality, and then deeper, and deeper, approaching the central event of a Draconian's existence: the neuter phase marking a watershed between male and female, active and passive.

Now Ian's voice grew hoarse; he took more and more time over each successive answer, hunting for words, repeating himself and then declaring that was wrong and trying again and once continuing for five or six minutes with a series of wild surrealist images, while his face twisted into a mask of agony and tears leaked from his closed lids.

"What's hurting him so?" Rorschach whispered when Lucas had instructed Ian to relax for a bit following that long, slow, exhausting utterance.

"It's too early to be sure," Lucas answered equally softly. "My guess is that we've tapped into a personal problem—not related to the Draconians, but to Ian himself—which could have given him the clue he was after, or alternatively might have coloured a hallucination and lent it the spurious air of rationality."

"What sort of personal problem?"

"Sexual? Social? Your guess is as good as mine. You know he was orphaned when he was eight, of course. Perhaps being alone in the Ash site, aware no matter how he tried to ignore the knowledge that the city was doomed, or perhaps because his rather peculiar cast of mind has made him a solitary person and he resents this handicap—whatever the cause, it's clear he's attained an incredible degree of identification with our hypothetical version of the natives. He looks a little better now. I'll push on."

But not long after he resumed the interrogation, he had to break off again because Ian was clenching his fists and declaring flatly that he was going to die and it was all for nothing and he'd been stupid and wasn't fit to survive anyhow and . . .

Lucas soothed him back into deep trance and ordered him to rest until he wanted to wake up naturally. Then he gave Rorschach a despondent glance.

"Well?"

"That last bit," Rorschach said glumly. "It didn't sound very promising, did it?"

"No. Of course it's premature to say so, but I felt my hopes completely dashed by it. It was as though what he imagined to be an insight into the fate of the Draconians was no more than a renewed realisation, in the context of this ingenious artificial personality, that the species was indeed doomed to extinction."

Lucas stretched; he was stiff from long sitting on his stool face to face with Ian.

"Of course I'll keep on trying. I'll put him through at least a dozen sessions before I give up."

Rorschach rose and wandered to the window. Gazing out, eyes narrowed against the sunlight, he said with his back turned to Lucas, "Tell me, have you felt that things have been going wrong since we brought Ian back?"

"Very much so," Lucas said.

"How does it look to you?"

"It's hard to pin down, but . . . Oh, mostly there's a sense of fatigue. When we started out, we were always buoyant because every day saw some new discovery, and some new idea always boiled up at the monthly conferences, which enabled people to go away and put yet another theory to the test. That's changed, inevitably. We were on the brink of despondency when Cathy and Igor located the four temples—or whatever they are—and that gave us a fresh lease of life. But even that really spectacular discovery hasn't furnished us with all the stimulus we need. We're back to the regular grind, comparing scraps of data one by one, and now we have so much more information, so many more possible combinations, it's making us dreadfully tired."

Rorschach nodded. "Yes, that's part of it, I'm sure. One has noticed how, because Ian has generated several of the most recent new ideas, people are starting to pin their hopes on him. Without his connivance, of course. And when he actually set out on his venture at Ash, there was this slight but definite slackening in other people's efforts, as though they honestly expected him to come back with the complete solution. . . . There's one other crucial factor operating, though."

Lucas hesitated. He said eventually, "The fact that we're past the halfway mark of the current tour."

Rorschach exhaled gustily. "Thank goodness I'm not the only person who's noticed. I haven't dared mention it before in case it was illusory. After all, on previous tours we haven't had any sense of—of watershed, if you follow me."

Lucas sat down on a nearby bench, his legs dangling.

"True, true. But never before has the ship brought someone empowered to close the base and abolish the Starflight Fund."

"But we sorted that out!" Rorschach said sharply. "Thanks to Ian—" He broke off, his mouth rounding into an O.

"*That's* why everyone is developing this absurd reliance on Ian," Lucas said with a nod. "Not just his ideas, useful and original though they are. People are aware, even without realising, that quite unintentionally Ian made the difference between continuance of the base and evacuation to Earth. This sense of dependence is bound to grow worse as time goes by."

Rorschach was silent a long moment. Finally he said, "And if the ship doesn't come back . . . ?"

"I don't know." Lucas bit his lip. "But you may wager that you and I are not the only people wondering about that. I—uh—happened to be checking out some computer files the other day, and I noticed you'd been reviewing and updating the long-term survival programmes."

Rorschach said defensively, "It struck me as about time."

"Quite right. They haven't been revised since the end of the first tour, have they? I mean, bar the automatic inclusion of data concerning new arrivals. And I must say that even with your recent additions they don't look promising."

"No, they don't." Rorschach scowled. "In the first instance, all they were designed to do was keep us alive if the ship had an accident and its return was delayed for some fairly long period, a couple of extra years. Turning them into a blueprint for the permanent colonisation of this planet by human beings is a hell of a tough job. For one thing our gene pool, filtered through the available fertile women, is—" He broke off, obviously annoyed with himself.

Lucas rose and came to put his arm companionably around the older man's shoulders.

"Someone's got to face it sooner or later, Valentine. Someone has to take the cold-blooded calculations the machines make on our behalf and use them to help us face the idea that the ship may never come back. As director, I'm afraid it's up to you. I sympathise. Count on me for any help I can offer."

Behind them Ian stirred. They turned in time to see him rise, licking his lips.

"Did you . . . ?" he asked, and his voice failed him, while eager expectation lighted his eyes.

"Sorry," Lucas said. "Not yet. But we'll try again tomorrow."

"What's the problem? I *know* I had it all clear in my mind!"

"Yes, but . . ." Lucas sought for words. "Maybe it made sense in Draconian terms. What we have to do is find a way of translating them into human language, isn't it?" He smiled reassurance. "We'll try again tomorrow, shall we?"

"I guess so," Ian said dully. "Okay. If anybody wants me, I'll be in the refectory. I need a drink."

XVIII

Ian sat miserable at his bench in the relic shed, staring at the screen of the computer remote. On it stark letters and symbols reported the result of his latest search through the known patterns imprinted on the Draconian crystals.

They *were* fundamentally identical. Checking and double-checking designed to eliminate random noise due to the weight of overlay activating the piezo effect in them, which were supposed to make the differences clearer, had done the opposite. It had shown that what differences might once have existed between one crystal and its neighbour had been so slight the mere passage of time had blurred them past recovery.

"It's insane!" he said to the air. "Thousands and thousands and thousands of them, and all alike as peas! *Why?* We make identical objects, but for use—tools, coins, garments, practical things that are needed by vast numbers of people. An archeologist digging the ruins of Earth would find them scattered almost from pole to pole, not stacked up exclusively in huge central warehouses. And I was so close to understanding what they're for, so damnably close!"

He broke off, guiltily aware that it was unhealthy to address himself aloud in this fashion, but tempted to do so in another way. He resisted the temptation for a few seconds, then yielded with a sigh, and pressed a switch which wiped the screen and instead activated a speaker linked to the computers.

Once again—for the tenth, twelfth time?—he heard the recording made of his last session under hypnosis with Lucas, the one which

had reduced him to such a state of hysteria that Rorschach had forbidden him to try again.

Gabbling pure nonsense, even to his own ears, he heard his voice
made harsh by anger and sour by grief. What the hell could he possibly have meant by a phrase like "We all shrank until we didn't
have room for ourselves" or, weirder still, "We got fined and that
was the end of us!"?

Behind him there was a light footfall. He slapped the switch and
the recording stopped instantly, but it was too late. The newcomer
was Cathy, and she was predictably annoyed.

"Ian, when you are going to stop this foolishness?" she demanded.
"You've listened to that until you must know it by heart, but every
time I come in I seem to find you at it again!"

Without looking at her, he retorted, "You don't believe me any
more than the rest of them, do you? You don't believe I really understood, just for a fraction of a second, what exterminated the
Draconians!"

"Of course," Cathy said. "I've said I take your word for it, haven't
I? But until you—"

Now he swung around on his chair to face her, eyes blazing.
"I'm getting sick of the way people are treating me!" he exploded.

Seeming frightened, she stepped back half a pace. "What do you
mean?" she countered.

"You know damn' well—or at any rate you should! It's plain
enough, isn't it?" He jumped to his feet and began to stride up and
down, pounding fist into palm to emphasise his words.

"Everybody's acting as though I've—I've betrayed them! Just because Lucas isn't smart enough to take me back under hypnosis to
the stage I reached when he was idiotic enough to drag me away
from Ash! Is it my fault that I was interrupted just at the crucial
moment? Is it my fault that Rorschach refuses to give me back the
simulacrum, so I can have another go? Well, is it?"

He glared at her.

Timidly she said, "Ian, you're letting this prey on your mind.
I'm sure nobody thinks you've let us down."

"That's what you think, is it? Well, you damn' well ought to
open your eyes and ears! Stop humouring me! Stop making soothing

noises to calm me down! Get a grip on what's actually happening
for a change!"

She looked at him levelly, her face pale.

"Ian, why is it that every time I try to discuss this with you ra-
tionally you break out into a hysterical rage?"

"I do not!"

"Listen to yourself, Ian. Do it on tape, if you have to, but listen.
You're disappointed, naturally, but instead of working to put things
right you're making them worse. You ought to be consulting people
instead of insulting them!"

He closed the gap between them with a single long stride and
slapped her cheek with a sound like a gunshot.

Instantly he could have cut off his hand. He stood frozen, watching the paleness of her skin give way to red where he had struck
her. She made as though to touch her cheek in disbelief, but cancelled the impulse and lowered her arm again.

Her tone measured, she said, "You're not being the Ian I fell in
love with. When you get back to where you were, let me know. But
for the time being I don't want any more to do with you."

She spun on her heel and stalked away. The door slammed.
When he ran after her, shouting, she ignored him, and when he
returned to the room they had been sharing, he found everything
that belonged to her had been removed.

"Ian?"

A soft voice pierced the midnight darkness. He was sitting alone
on a rock, half a mile from the base, at the edge of the glass disc
into which the first arrivals had sterilised the sand. He didn't look
around; he was staring, unseeing, at the heedless stars.

It was cold. Here as on Earth it was always cold at night in a
desert. But he didn't pay attention to that, either.

The voice belonged to Igor. Shortly, his dark lean figure appeared
from the direction of the base, his feet making little crunching
noises.

"I won't ask if you mind my joining you," he said. "But I propose
to do so anyhow."

There was another rock nearby, of a convenient height for sitting on. He moved towards it. Sat. Did something Ian could not make out. Then, abruptly, a flame loomed hurtfully bright, there were sucking sounds, and a waft of smoke reached Ian's nostrils.

He said involuntarily, "A pipe?"

Igor chuckled. "Ah, you haven't lost your tongue. . . . Yes, a pipe. I brought it from Earth more as a souvenir than for use. I suppose this is—oh—the fourth time I've lit it since I arrived."

The red glow of the pipe bowl was just enough to show his sharp features when he drew on it.

"Hmm!" he commented after a pause. "Synthetic it may be, but it's convincingly like tobacco. Perhaps a bit harsh—like you."

"I guess you've been talking to Cathy," Ian said bitterly.

"No, right now Cathy isn't talking to anybody," Igor murmured. "And so far as I'm concerned what's happened between you is none of my business. I'm sorry about it, but that doesn't give me the right to interfere. Not unless you, as a friend, invite me to mediate . . . which I'd cheerfully do, of course. I was very pleased when you and she got together."

Ian didn't answer. Having drawn twice more on his pipe and tamped the mock tobacco with a handy pebble, Igor resumed, "Still, that's not why I came out looking for you. I suddenly wanted to ask you why you became involved in archeology."

"What?"

"Does it sound like a silly question? I guess it may. . . . But I've been thinking a lot about my own motives recently. You know, we've got to face the fact, sooner or later, that the *Stellaris* may have made her last voyage. Something may all too easily have gone wrong on Earth which has destroyed the—what's the term?—the infrastructure she depends on. Thinking about the all too real possibility that I may die here and never see my home again, I started wondering what led me to another planet."

He puffed reflectively.

"I very nearly became a mineralogist, you know, rather than an archeologist. I'd almost completed my training, when my wife and my baby daughter were killed in an accident, and the shock drove me into a nervous breakdown. It took me three years to get over it."

"I didn't know!" Ian exclaimed, startled out of his apathy.

Igor sighed. "Yes, I did ask them not to include that in the briefing tapes at Starflight Centre. It was a long time ago—thirty years—and I'm not the same person as I was then. But, as I was going to say: for a long time I believed that that was why I switched to archeology. I suspected myself of wanting to recover the past I'd set such store by, snatched away from me by blind chance. It wasn't until I'd spent a long time here that I realised the impulse was deeper, and more subtle."

The pipe was burning badly; he fumbled on the ground for the handy stone and retamped the bowl.

"What was it?" Ian said slowly.

"The fact that I'm a Pole," Igor answered. "Citizen of a country which for centuries didn't exist. Yet it was, in the end, re-created, and continues to this day. I believe now that my subconscious argument went like this: For my ancestors, proud of their heritage, there was a time when they were afraid their homeland had disappeared forever. Nonetheless, they refused to accept that idea, and worked until it was proved false. In my personal case, I imagined I had no reason to go on living; in fact I did once try to kill myself. Then I realised that that was absurd. I could make a new and very good life, and devote it to—what can I call it?—the creation of a link between the past and the future, that bond which so often seems to have been severed and in fact cannot be no matter how much strain is put on it."

"I think I understand that," Ian said after pondering for a while.

"I would expect you to. With a name like yours I take it your ancestors were Scottish even though you were born half a world away."

"Yes, of course."

"I've been to the Scottish islands, the Hebrides. As a matter of fact, I went there deliberately just before I reported to join *Stellaris*. Have you ever been there?"

Ian was jolted. He said in sheer amazement, "Yes, and—and for the same reason!"

"The idea was planted in your mind. I arranged for it to be planted."

"What?"

"I'd never met you, but I was sure that somebody who had such strong involvement with the past would be deeply affected by seeing those abandoned settlements, the crofts open to the wind, the land that once was ploughed and sown returned to the weeds and the wild grasses. . . ." Igor gestured with his pipe. "I went there because I wanted to feel what it was like to walk among ruins left by people who cared little or nothing for written records, who lived their lives and vanished into the anonymous dark. I had my choice of a score of islands where the same thing has happened, but I decided I should choose a place which the classical historians described as lying on the dark and misty edge of the world, where sky and sea blend into a confusion neither one thing nor the other. I thought it might have the same impact on you, only maybe stronger, you being of Scottish descent. Do you feel you've been manipulated?"

Ian hesitated. Suddenly he gave a harsh laugh. "In a way. But it's nothing I can resent. It makes me—well, it makes me admire you more than I already did."

"The admiration is mutual," Igor said. "And it's not at all affected by what you persist in regarding as your recent failure. It was a colossal—a fantastic—success. I couldn't have done it. Nobody else here could have done it."

"It wasn't a success!" Ian burst out. "It could have been, only—"

"Only someone was stupid enough to save your life." Igor inserted the words with the precision of a surgeon's knife. "You shortsighted fool. What good would it have done the rest of us if you'd discovered the secret and nursed it into your grave—hm?"

"I . . ." Ian bit his lip, and eventually nodded.

"Good. Now we're getting somewhere. I know exactly the predicament you're in; it's happened to me time and again, not in connection with inscriptions because that's not my speciality, but in connection with artefacts. What's this corroded lump here, then? I think it's a—a—a . . . ! Just a moment! And then the moment stretches into weeks, months, sometimes years, and one day when I've almost forgotten about it: click! Of course! That ridiculous Y-shaped bit of metal can only have been a cramp for plough handles made from unplaned tree branches! That's a real example, by the way. Another that I was nearly as proud of was one time when I realised that a fascinating artefact dug up at a site in Crete actually must have been left behind by a Victorian archeological expedition."

"You're joking!"

"Not at all. But I'd never have caught on if I hadn't recognised a drawing of it in a magazine advertisement from 1898." Igor chuckled, drew one final time on his pipe, and tapped out the dottle against the rock he was sitting on.

"What I'm counselling you, Ian, is simply patience. I'd never have mentioned that I planted the suggestion of your trip to the Hebrides, but that I wanted to impress you with my—shall I call it my right? Yes, that's accurate—my *right*, then, to give you advice. I say that what you should do is go back to your quarters and get some sleep, and in the morning make it up with Cathy, because you two working together are more than the sum of your parts, and stop imagining that you're infallible simply because you're a hell of a sight smarter than six of the rest of us rolled into one."

"I never—"

"Yes you did. Stop it."

Ian licked his lips. "Is that really the impression I give people?"

"Only when you're very angry with yourself. And you've no call for that, on your showing up to now. Come on, let's walk back together."

Igor took the younger man companionably by the arm and led him away.

XIX

Talking to Igor was like having mist cleared from his mind by a sea-fresh breeze. The more he thought over what the older man had said, the more Ian realised he was absolutely right.

Okay, so I came up with a handful of bright new ideas on my very first tour! But so did almost everybody else! And no doubt all the others also vainly hoped they'd be the first to solve the mystery. . . .

He sought out Cathy and surprised himself by being able to apologise in a few short, sincere words; all too often, when it came to expressing his deepest feelings, he waffled and mumbled and went all around Robin Hood's barn. Her answer was typically direct.

"Good. I'm glad. See you tonight."

As though his mental mist had been veiling things he ought to have spotted long ago, he suddenly found he was able to review with detachment a whole range of possibilities that might lead him back on a conscious, human level to the forgotten insight he'd experienced at Ash. He sat down and worked out a careful list of subjects, and then systematically set about interrogating his colleagues on each in turn.

Nadine Shah was busy in the bio lab conducting a series of comparison tests on genetic material recovered from the most recent of the Draconian corpses embalmed by anaerobic water at the peat site, checking the gene equivalents one by one against a range of cells from contemporary fauna. But most of the job was being done by the computers, so she was quite happy to spend a while chatting with Ian.

"I've been thinking back over the summary of our ideas about the Draconians which Igor gave to Ordoñez-Vico," he began. "I didn't think about it at the time since palaeobiology of course is not my speciality, but now I'm struck by one astonishing omission."

"That being . . . ?"

"He made no mention of natural population-control processes as a possible explanation for the natives' extinction."

Nadine gave a wry smile. "I'm afraid that's not astonishing at all," she said. "I don't imagine you dug that far back into the computer stores, but of course a population collapse was among the first ideas that were exhaustively evaluated by the original party here. In fact I spent the first couple of months after I arrived double-checking some work that Ruby Ngola had done on population-control forces." She was referring to one of the people who had been rotated home last time the *Stellaris* called. "Attractive and logical though the suggestion was, we had to rule it out—categorically and once for all. And everything we've learned since confirms that we were right to do so. If you want the full details, I can put them up on a screen for you, but I suspect some of the equations we use may be a little hard for a nonspecialist to follow."

"Give it to me in words, then," Ian invited.

"Oh, essentially it's very simple. Short of significant climatic changes, or the appearance of some brand-new mutation, populations here are a hell of a lot more stable than their counterparts on Earth. There's an incredibly close match, for example, between the number of young born in a good year and in a bad year. When more fodder is available, more active males are competing for the sessile females, but by the same token they're also better able to drive one another away. When there's little food to be had, the males become less active and just about the same number of females get fertilised. Where an earthly population may fluctuate by several hundred per cent, a boom followed by a crash, herd size here generally remains within a range of plus or minus six to eight per cent. Granted, it's obvious that the Draconians interfered with the natural order, but it's been proved that they expanded steadily, moving constantly into new territory, at a rate that corresponds very well with the maximum speed of population increase in contemporary species. So, unless it was the shock of meeting themselves coming back, as it were . . ." She grinned broadly.

But Ian was frowning. "Yes, I see. They didn't even occupy all the regions of their planet which would have been comfortable for them, did they?"

"That's right, they didn't. So unless some areas were out of bounds to them because of something we don't know about— endemic disease, perhaps—they would still have had enough food and enough territory to at least double their numbers without feeling the pinch. By the way, when I said we dismissed the idea completely, I don't mean we've ignored it; we have a monitor programme constantly sifting new data to see if there's any reason for changing our minds. But it's been—oh—five years since that programme called for attention, and then it was a false alarm."

"Thanks very much," Ian said, and rose to go.

The next person he inquired of was Ruggiero Bono, as being their leading authority on the natives' palaeotechnology. He cornered the little dark man in the refectory after the evening meal, and asked whether, if the natives used bioelectronic devices, they could ever have developed a self-perpetuating strain of something that broadcast so loud a signal it interfered with their sensory perceptions and maybe even with their thinking.

"Hmm!" Ruggiero rubbed his chin. "You mean some kind of weed that would—well—deafen them?"

"That's more or less the idea."

"Just a second. . . ." Ruggiero produced his pocket calculator and ran his fingers over it, frowning. Eventually he shook his head.

"Sorry, no. It's a clever notion, but quite impossible. There simply couldn't be that much energy in a vegetable metabolism. The poor plant would curl up and frizzle at the edges. And in any case, if that were the explanation, tell me please why they were all affected by it, including the ones far enough away from the spot where the problem arose to have time to take steps and put it right!"

"Good point," Ian muttered ruefully. "Well, then, have you come across any relics, any artefacts, which might indicate that they were changing over from organic to inorganic devices? I imagine a human-built radio, or indeed a good few of our own gadgets, would have driven a Draconian instantly insane."

"Oh, that's perfectly true," Ruggiero conceded. "An output of twenty watts would have hurt them terribly—but I don't have to tell you that, after your experience in the simulacrum. But the answer's no, again. Sorry to disappoint you. So far as we can tell, their crowning achievement was to visit the moon and build their scope up there. If they were still using bioelectronics for that, then they almost certainly were not changing over to inorganics."

"Just a second," Ian said. "Would those bioelectronics have been capable of emitting signals powerful enough to be heard down here?"

"I see what you're driving at," Ruggiero muttered, his eyes fixed on nowhere. "That would argue a very powerful signal indeed, which brings us back to your first question, doesn't it? But . . . Well, if you like I'll check out what the computers have to say on the subject, but I'm inclined to suspect first of all that you could do things in vacuum which you couldn't do here in a humid atmosphere, and second that they probably went up and down to collect the data. Consider: that flying machine, that one sunken ship! To me it seems more consonant with their ordinary behaviour to assume that they had one and only one moonship—just as we have one starship!—and shuttled back and forth, making their mistakes, if any, on the very first trip and thereafter treating it as a matter of routine. You know we haven't dug up anything resembling a spaceport."

He hesitated. "Funny! I never looked at it quite that way before: they had one moonship, most likely, and we haven't found it; we have one starship. And that may not come back, either."

"I suspect you're about to become dismal," Ian said. "Have another glass of wine."

The next person he tackled was Achmed Hossein. The lean, beak-nosed Arab gravely considered the question of whether, in the light of information theory, it might be possible for an interaction between members of the Draconian species that was in fact insane to be so total that no single member of the race escaped.

He thought for a moment, and then said, "Ian, I'll give you this. You never stop trying, do you? I'm not sure I can answer with authority, but at least it's a brand-new suggestion and we're running terribly short of those."

He swung around in his chair and punched the keyboard of the nearest computer read-in.

For a while there was no sound bar the faint electrical hum of the machines in the computer hall.

Then, studying a series of figures as they appeared on the screen above the read-in, he said, "A shame. There literally isn't one chance in a million of a contagious psychosis being spread by that mode of contact. Not even if the person who went insane had the greatest charisma in all space and all time. We know the effective limit of the electrical senses of contemporary species—that's what I punched for first—and we know the probable attenuation factor of a real-time signal, and we know a good few other relevant items. What emerges is something like an epidemic pattern; given that the disease is capable of infecting the species, it must *a priori* be similar enough to previous diseases for certain individuals to possess antibodies endowing them with at least partial resistance. There will always be some survivors, and the odds are all in favour of there being a number of total-immunes. Same goes for this notion of a contagious form of insanity. By the time it had been filtered through a few dozen contacts, it would be attenuated. Overprinted, as it were, with more normal mental attitudes. It could destroy a small community, but not the entire race."

He leaned back. "What's more, the sort of ultra-violent psychosis you're talking about would probably have made the victim nonviable. He'd have—oh!—forgotten to eat!"

Ian said thoughtfully, "I'd more or less worked that out myself, given that we believe the Draconians communicated by externalising patterns that corresponded to internal bodily states. I'd hazard a guess that they probably never treated mental illness—merely ostracised the sufferer—and that was why I came and asked you about contagion. Like you say, though, the odds are all in favour of someone that deranged being incapable of functioning like a proper person. It would more likely kill a few individuals than all of them. Oh, well . . . !"

Achmed gave an airy wave. "Sorry to disappoint you! But if you come up with any more fresh approaches, let me know. Things are becoming terribly dull around here, aren't they? You seem to be the only person still firing on all cylinders."

When Cathy next returned from her twenty-day spell of duty at the peat site, after the enjoyable reunion of their lovemaking, they lay side by side for a long while, not speaking.

"You're very quiet," Cathy said at last.

"So are you."

"Yes. . . . But nothing very much has happened at the site, you know. We just keep shifting cover and inspecting what we find underneath, and there isn't anything as startling as the temples for us to report on this time."

"You haven't figured out any new explanations for those damn' things, have you?"

"None at all. Four mysteries wrapped inside four puzzles and four enigmas! You?"

"I do seem to be producing ideas again," Ian said wryly. "In fact Achmed said I'm the only person who is around here. I've just been tackling people, one by one, as I work down a list of possibilities, some ridiculous, some promising, not one fruitful. . . . But I haven't reached the end of the list yet. There's still hope."

Once more there was a period of silence. Suddenly Cathy said, "Speaking of hope, Ian: do you think there's any hope that the *Stellaris* will come back?"

He was so startled, he rose on one elbow to stare at her even though the room was in darkness.

"Why in hell do you ask that?" he demanded.

"Because . . ." She hesitated. "Because if she doesn't, it will be the women who have to worry most, won't it?"

"Oh!" Ian sounded dismayed. "Yes, I see what you mean!"

"If the ship doesn't arrive," Cathy went on doggedly, "we shall presumably have to choose between suicide and trying to set up a permanent colony. I'm not the suicidal type, but on the other hand I'm not the maternal type, either. Sometimes, out at the dig, I've lain awake for hours, wondering whether I can face the job of bearing and raising children so that mankind can survive here when—for all we can tell—it hasn't survived on its native planet."

Chidingly he said, "But you're talking as though the ship has already failed to come back!"

"Time's wasting," Cathy muttered. "We'll know soon—in a matter of a few more months. Wouldn't it be terrible if we did fathom the mystery of the Draconians and then sat here, waiting, forever and a day because on Earth they'd lost interest or smashed things up so badly they couldn't afford to send the ship here again?"

"It won't happen," Ian said, trying to sound confident. "Out of the question! Even if there were—oh—a war, or something, the mere fact that people have been sent here would be enough to make them want to re-establish contact."

"Garbage."

"What?"

"I said garbage! I'm talking about the kind of war which would make it literally impossible to contact us again."

"Well . . ." He lay down anew. "Well, yes. There is that."

"Of course there is. And nothing we do can make any difference. I guess we'd better try to go to sleep. But if I wake up screaming, you'll know what I've been dreaming about."

X X

Item by item Ian ticked off his list, but it seemed to remain the same length as it was originally; every time he had to consign an idea to oblivion, another struck him. It would be a miracle if that process continued for more than a few more weeks; still, while it lasted, it was comforting.

He went to call on Karen at the civil engineering headquarters, where she was supervising the manufacture of a new batch of girders to be shipped to Peat and riveted together in order to hold back a wall of soft crumbly vegetable matter that threatened to slump down and bury the digging machines.

"Well, hello stranger!" Karen said in a friendly mocking tone as he entered her office, three-parts walled with tinted glass that allowed her to watch the foundry processes directly as well as monitoring them by way of the electronic systems. "I thought we weren't pals any more!"

"Lord, has it become that bad?" Ian said in near dismay . . . but a second later he caught on, and was grinning as he sat down in a vacant chair beside her, without waiting for an invitation. "Can I interrupt?"

"Talk all you like. This is going very smoothly."

"Well, what it boils down to is this. It just occurred to me that while almost everybody else keeps offering theories about the fate of the Draconians, you don't. And you're here, and you have a speciality that's very important to us, and—well, do you have any new suggestions?"

"That's a brute of a question!" She spun around in her chair and looked keenly at him. "The main reason nobody asked me before, I dare say, is because it's out of my field. I make things. I'm practical, not theoretical."

"Then make me a practical suggestion, why not?"

Karen chuckled. "Okay! After all, I've been here as long as you, and I must have thought of something by now, even if other people already decided it wasn't worth consideration. . . . I take it you've been through the biological and psychological bit, and you want me to see if I can think of a material, inorganic idea?"

"I'd welcome one. I'm not well grounded in that area."

"Me, yes—but as to how a mineral salt or something contaminating water could have affected a Draconian . . . Well, I did once think of a point I don't believe has been discussed at a monthly conference, though I'm sure it must have been investigated by Nadine or Lucas."

"You'd be surprised at what we've overlooked. Even though it turned out not to be important when we did finally evaluate it."

"Okay." Karen shrugged, making her large soft body ripple like a disturbed pond. "Among the things they tell you when you're training to design like a new city in an underdeveloped region is what may well have rendered the Roman upper classes decadent. Not only did they pipe their water by lead conduits—they also liked to ferment their wine in lead-lined vats because that made it sweeter. If you ever looked into primitive chemistry or alchemy, you probably ran across the ancient term 'sugar of lead,' which is a lead-salt that oddly enough tastes sweet."

"You're saying the Draconians might have let some insidious poison build up in their bodies?"

"Don't ask me, ask a biologist—and right now, excuse me, please, because I think we've got an overheat in Number Nine solar furnace which is on the way to melting the wrong things!"

Nadine and Lucas were polite, but perceptibly scornful, and dashed his hopes. Naturally, any buildup of poisonous metal— whether light, like beryllium, or heavy, like lead or mercury—would have been revealed when they were running element checks on the

first corpses to be dug up. Neither those nor any more recent speci-
mens had shown signs of poison; the last remaining, very slender,
possibility consisted in some organic poison like DDT which time
had dissociated into its simpler molecules . . . but that was out of
reach forever if it had existed.

Scrub another bright idea.

Meantime, he received uniformly doleful reports from the computer in which he had left running a programme to clarify and
analyse the patterns in the printed crystals. No matter whether
the data came from remotes at the digs, "reading" the crystals as they
were found in one "library" after another—at least one per city-site,
and at Peat and Ash two—or whether they came from crystals he
had brought to the base with care in nonmagnetic padded crates,
they all converged towards a single conclusion.

*Damn it, they did make thousands and maybe millions of the
things printed with patterns so nearly identical as to be indistin-
guishable now!*

Olaf and Sue had temporarily turned over Ash to the automatics
when a library was found, at long last, in the Silt city. Ian borrowed
a hovercraft and went out to look it over. Small wonder, though,
that it hadn't been spotted before; so much weight had overlain the
building where the crystals had been stored, the piezo effect had
randomised the information beyond recall. Besides, when the site
was underwater—probably for about fifteen thousand years—electrical fields due to sea creatures had also taken their toll.

It was raining when Ian first clapped eyes on that particular library: rack after stack of crystals were being laid bare to the downpour by the automatics. At random he said to his companions, "Hey,
can you think of any reason to make so many identical entries in an
information store?"

They both glanced at him in surprise. He went on rather sheep-
ishly, "See, I came here to try to read what's—what's written in these
things. I didn't really have much hope of success, but I didn't expect,
either, that I couldn't come up with any explanation for their existence!"

"You said something at the last monthly conference," Sue recalled with a frown, "about the differences between them being so slight. . . ."

Olaf snapped his fingers. "I know where you find lots of virtually identical records!"

"What?" Ian looked as though he wanted to embrace Olaf. "Tell me, quick!"

"Well, in a government office, right? I mean, like a tax collector's or a birth-and-death registrar's. . . ." Olaf's eyes grew round in wonder at his own perceptivity. "Say, I believe I just hit on something, didn't I?"

"You certainly did," Ian said with feeling. "And I've just realised there's somebody I haven't pestered with my questions when I ought to have."

The others looked a question at him.

"Valentine Rorschach, damn it!" Ian exploded. "We've been deep, deep into the bodily functions and the nervous system and the sexual habits and whatever of the natives, and we've neglected the holistic aspect of their society. We've never asked whether they had a government, and if so, how it could have operated."

"I'll be damned," Sue said in pure wonderment. "You go beard Valentine and see what he can bring up for us at the next conference, hear?"

Rorschach looked faintly surprised when—after false starts due to excitement—Ian managed to put his point over.

"It honestly never occurred to me before," he said, "but you're right. They picked me to come here because they thought I'd be a competent director, not because I'm outstanding in any single scientific field like Igor or Lucas. But it's true that every skill on the planet is precious, and I probably ought to have applied mine to the study of the natives as well. . . . On the other hand: how could any—what would you call it?—any administrative problem lead to the extinction of a species?"

"I don't know," Ian admitted at once. "But I can tell you this. No other suggestion put to me has come closer to touching me on the spot where I felt the—the raw hurt of impending doom when I was exploring Ash in the simulated Draconian."

Rorschach pursed his lips. "I don't know whether to say that's interesting, or that's reassuring, or that's indicative. . . . Could you leave it with me for a day or two? I'll review every item I can find that might have a bearing on hypothetical social organisation among the natives, and see if anything significant comes out."

"That'll be fine," Ian said, and rose to leave. Rorschach checked him.

"Since you're here, Ian, I ought to take advantage of the opportunity. . . . I'm not sure how best to put this, but I imagine you, like most of us, have been wondering what will happen if *Stellaris* fails to turn up on schedule?"

Ian lowered himself slowly back into his chair. He said after a miniature eternity, "Yes. Cathy and I talked about that already."

"Good; I can save the preamble for somebody else. I was expecting that." Rorschach licked his lips. "I know it's very cold-blooded, but we are compelled to think—if worse comes to worst—in terms of genetic pools and optimal unions and rhesus negative and—"

"What you're driving at," Ian broke in, "is that we shall have to work out a plan to establish ourselves permanently."

"The plans don't have to be worked out. They've existed since the base was set up. The chance of our being stranded has always been in the realm of possibility; now, though, it's attained probability in many people's minds. Have you noticed?"

Ian hesitated. Memories of casual, bitter remarks—like Ruggiero's of a few weeks ago—came back to him. He nodded.

"I think it's time I started making it clear to people that the failure of the *Stellaris* to arrive needn't mean the end of the universe," Rorschach said in a brittle, rehearsed-sounding voice. "We have an excellent spectrum of genetic endowment, and your heredity is among the finest on the planet. So is Cathy's. We'd appreciate it if—"

Ian was ahead of him. He said sharply, "If, when the crunch comes, we'd be the first to agree that we ought to start a family and make a bid for survival of the species."

Rorschach inclined his head.

"Precisely. But a little more than that. The first to agree that you'll share out your genes—spread them as far as possible among the next generation."

Ian looked at him for a long while. Eventually he said, cheeks very pale above his red beard, "I know why you had to say that, Valentine. I know it makes good sense. I'm sure Olaf and Sue and Karen and Achmed and everybody will be agreeable, and they wouldn't be here any more than myself or Cathy if their heredity weren't admirable. But I could wish that you'd prefaced that blunt remark with the answer to a question I imagine you know is bound to be asked."

Rorschach, face strained, gave a slow nod. "What's life going to be like among a group of thirty very independent, very intelligent people who came here for one special purpose and find that they're marooned with no way of letting Earth know even if that original goal is attained?"

"Exactly. It's not going to be much fun, is it?"

"No." For a fleeting instant the director looked old, far older than his actual age, as though his mind had been much preyed on by anxiety. "But there it is—and we may be wrong in taking these pessimistic precautions."

"I guess so."

"I hope so," Rorschach countered. "Keep it up on the level of hope as long as possible, hm?"

"Ah, Ian! Valentine tells me you've even cornered him now to kick him into a fresh appraisal of our problems!"

Beaming, Igor approached Ian in the refectory; both had arrived a few minutes early for the start of the monthly conference.

"What? Oh!" Ian gave a wry grin. "Really it was Olaf and Sue who put me on the track of that. And then Valentine promptly hit back with a real problem, something much worse than a mystery."

Igor's face became grave as he lowered himself into the adjacent chair.

"Yes, I know about that. We all do, I think. Even if we aren't discussing it openly. I'm sure you're taking it dispassionately for the time being at least, no matter how tough it may prove to be in the long run. Am I right in suspecting Cathy may be reacting the opposite way around?"

"You know her very well, don't you?"

"No." Igor shook his head. "Since—well, the tragedy I once described to you, I've been chary of overclose acquaintance with women. But I think I sum her up accurately."

Ian nodded, his eyes on Igor's face. He said after a pause, his voice strained, "We've talked about you a lot. She—I—what I mean is . . ." But the right phrase eluded him; he broke off.

"She—?" Igor said with deliberate obtuseness.

Ian drew a deep breath. "She said maybe her first child ought to be yours. Just in case, when it comes time for a second, you . . ."

"In case I'm too old," Igor said in a gravelly voice. And raised his hand to forestall Ian's ready contradiction. "Oh, don't try to deceive me. I could well be. Deprived of our contact with Earth, flimsy though that is, we could easily slip into a decline. What do you want me to say?"

"Nothing. I want to hear it, that's all."

"Then I'm flattered" was Igor's instant response. "More, perhaps, than ever in my life. How curious it is, though, to think of oneself as—as breeding stock! Isn't it *strange*? To have to shed thousands of years of preconceptions, a lifetime of social conditioning . . . But I guess it's true that we shall have to make the best of what we've got."

He stared at Ian, whose eyes had suddenly unfocussed and whose cheeks had turned paper-pale.

"Ian!" he exclaimed. "Is something the matter?"

"I . . ." Ian shook his head, as though giddy. "I don't know! But when you said that, I felt—I thought . . . Oh, *hell*! I don't know! Something came right to the tip of my tongue, and now it's gone again, and—"

And half a dozen other people came into the room and there were distractions on every side.

XXI

Slowly time wore away towards the scheduled date of the next visit by *Stellaris*. By stages the work at the various digs was cut back, so that there would be a chance to assess, review and digest what had been discovered during this two-year tour, and decisions could be reached concerning what artefacts should be shipped to Earth. Clearly, one of the most important items ought to be a statue; they settled on the second-least damaged of the group of four, and with utmost care dismounted it from its roof, loaded it on a hovercraft, brought it back to the base.

Encased in a transparent block of plastic, poured cold, to protect its delicate surface finish, it stood outside the puny human buildings, like the ghost of a giant, and seemed to mock without words.

Certainly there had been some spectacular finds since the ship last called. Equally certainly, each of them had made the mystery deeper. It burdened the minds of them all with gloom. To make sure that starflight would continue, to keep up the flagging interest of those at home, they had hoped to produce vast amounts of new positive knowledge. Instead, what they had learned was chiefly negative: that idea can be dismissed now, so can that, so can that. . . .

Depressed and resentful, the staff reassembled on the day appointed, and then began the time of fearful waiting. It had been bad last trip, Ian was told, when *Stellaris* was twelve whole days overdue; this time it was going to be infinitely worse even though she might be a mere one day late.

Rorschach, with the help of Igor and Lucas, kept trying to revive people's spirits by reminding them that Rudolf Weil had promised to devote all his efforts to ensuring that some kind of contact with Earth would be maintained at all costs. But his assurances rang hollow. The name of Ordoñez-Vico cropped up in conversation again, at first in passing, then as a central subject in an argument.

A myriad wild hypotheses flew from mouth to mouth: suppose there's been an all-out war at long last, suppose some terrorist group managed to sabotage the ship by smuggling a bomb up to her in a batch of supplies, suppose there's been a financial crash, worldwide, and the Starflight Fund has gone into bankruptcy, suppose the United Nations has collapsed owing to friction between competing nationalistic interests . . . !

Five days late; seven; ten—and the subject of conversation had altered again, this time to consideration of the ways in which they might survive here. Nobody wanted that. Nobody wanted to settle permanently on Sigma Draconis III, because they hadn't come here as colonists, but as investigators. Frequently people invoked Ian's experience when he was deciphering the Zimbabwe script: it was all very well for him to demonstrate that a modern man could still live the way an ancient tribe had lived, but would he have wanted to be condemned to that for the rest of his life—drinking foul water, eating what he could gather or kill with a snare or a spear, forever at the mercy of wild animals and strange disease?

There was an unprecedented run on the beer and wine programmes at the refectory.

Then, supported by hangovers, tempers began to flare; for the first time since the base was founded a fistfight broke out on the thirteenth day of waiting for the ship. Achmed, doing his best to keep his self-control despite the fact that he—as their communications chief—was the focus of all their vague, diffuse resentment, as though it was his fault the ship's signal had not appeared, had broached to Nadine Shah the possibility that they might have children together, as being the only two people here of Muslim extraction.

Ordinarily, matters of religious belief were left to one side among the base staff; the majority, perhaps twenty, of them had no faith, but of course when it came to raising children, with all the attendant questions of passing on a cultural tradition, subconscious reflexes entered into play, old habit patterns not thought about for years.

And when Achmed learned that Ruggiero, a Catholic, had made the same suggestion to Nadine—explosion. He broke Ruggiero's nose and lost a tooth.

As though frightened that they too might explode, people took to avoiding one another's company. Whereas last time, while waiting for the ship, most people had spent most of each day in the computer hall, chatting and hoping, now they drifted apart into small groups. If so many as six or seven people found themselves in the computer hall together, only a few minutes would pass before a couple of them would find a reason for moving elsewhere.

Even when it was mealtime, the refectory was never more than half full; some people came early, others, on seeing that ten or fifteen were already present, would decide to wait an extra half hour. In the evenings they dispersed to their quarters instead of staying together to talk, listen to music or play videotapes.

One could sense that if a colony were compulsorily set up on this planet, it would be fragmented before it came into existence.

The prospect was nothing short of terrifying.

Some few people, including Ian and Cathy, were not content to mooch around, but did their dogged best to concentrate on their work. The cataloguing of artefacts could be double-checked; the seemingly identical patterns printed in the Draconian crystals could be sifted again and yet again, in the hope that in some few of them might have survived the faint, faint resonances that must—*a priori* must!—once have distinguished each from its neighbours. After the fifteenth day Rorschach started encouraging others to do the same; after the twentieth, he was blunt about it, making it a near order, though carefully calculated not to appear an outright command.

It helped a little. For some people, though, there was nothing to do: Karen's civil engineers, in particular, had already checked and rechecked all their equipment, and Achmed and his computer-and-communications group were also in a boring, frustrating rut, obliged to keep watch for the ship by turns, and always being disappointed.

How long must they postpone the decision to face facts? How long before they set about a rational reorganisation on settlement lines, gave up their vain hope of hearing from Earth again?.

Ian put the question late one night to Cathy, and she shivered a little as she tried to answer.

"Ian, we're in a terrible double bind! All of us know that after waiting this long we may have to wait indefinitely—but when it comes to working out the pattern for a permanent colony, there are such hideous problems to be solved that we simply don't want to discuss them. There are physical problems, aren't there? Making the most of our gene pool, that's the worst because it means scrapping so many of our hopes, ambitions, preferences. . . ."

"Igor said how strange it is to have to think of oneself as breeding stock," Ian muttered.

"That's it exactly," Cathy said. "Beyond that, though, there are other subtler questions. Can children be raised healthy and intelligent on a diet provided by way of machines? Can we duplicate those machines when our population increases past the capacity of those we have? Can we be sure that a baby won't succumb to a disease that leaves an adult virtually unaffected? Beyond that again there are the psychological problems; we just had an example when Achmed attacked Ruggiero. What sort of society are we going to devise? It's a horrible responsibility, isn't it? Are we going to try to make a kind of tribal structure, or are we going to fall into old patterns for the sake of their familiarity? Are we going to be communist or capitalist, are we going to be individualistic or egalitarian, are we going to introduce money or some other kind of comparative scale of entitlement to what there is, are we going to have to evaluate people and say this person gets more than that person of what's available?"

"You've thought this through very deeply, haven't you?" Ian said.

"So have you. And probably Valentine has worked it out in even more detail than the rest of us. It goes without saying that if he'd figured out a solution, even one that was halfway tolerable, he wouldn't be letting us drift the way we are—snapping, backbiting, fretting all the time."

"I wonder how much longer it can last."

"Not very long. Something will have to be done, and soon."

And was, on the thirtieth day of waiting for the ship.

By now, Ian was getting accustomed to the new situation, and that head of his which—so long ago, so far away, in what felt like another universe—he had compared to a haunted house was once again humming with ideas. It was a vast relief to have something fresh to think about. He spent a long time walking around and around the statue of the Draconian in its plastic case, as though he could read the answer from its curious anomalous surface finish, that gave back such distorted electrical responses. Over and over the same obsessive phrases revolved in his mind:

To be rewarded. Division of labour. Make the best of what we've got.

But he couldn't be sure whether those related to the vanished natives, to his experience at Ash when wearing the Draconian simulacrum or to the plight of the humans.

Until, all of a sudden, when he woke on the thirtieth morning it was clear in his mind. He leapt from bed, not stopping longer than was needed to fling on his clothes, and ran from the room heedless of Cathy's cries.

Did I dream it? Did it come together because I slept on it so often? Doesn't matter! All that does matter is to find out whether the machines agree that that's the way it could have happened!

Feverish with excitement, hands shaking so much he could barely plan their movements across the computer read-in at the relic shed—which he had headed for by reflex born of familiarity, not because it was the nearest—he punched item after item of data into a new programme, gave it the necessary parameters concerning time and geographical distribution and genetic resources and—

"Ian, what are you doing?" Cathy called from the door, hurrying towards him.

"Shut up!" he snapped, and went on adding to the programme:

incidence of variation in the plants dug up from Peat, contrasts between the gene equivalents in the oldest and the most recent corpses, with special reference to the gravid female whose deformed baby was never born—

"Ian!"

"*Shut up!*" he shouted again, and then, relenting, said in a milder tone, "No, please don't interrupt. If you want to be useful, you could bring me some breakfast from the refectory—coffee and a roll or something of that kind."

"What's so important? What have you come up with?"

"I'll give you three guesses. And if you possess your soul in patience for an hour or two, I'll be able to tell you if I'm right or wrong."

There was a moment of dead silence. Then she said, "Ian, you haven't cracked it, have you? The language, I mean."

"No, but I think I figured out where we went astray. Go on, get me that coffee! It's bound to take me awhile before I pack everything relevant into this programme. Hurry and I may still be at it when you come back."

She spun on her heel and ran for the door.

When she returned, he was indeed still at it, and without looking around said, "Did I refer to an hour or two? It's going to be more like several hours. I keep coming up with things that might possibly fit, so I'll have to write them in, too."

Clearing a space on the workbench beside him so that she could set down the mug of coffee, she said, "But Valentine wants everybody in the refectory right away. He plans to hold a day-long discussion of our prospects."

"Carry on without me," Ian grunted. "I'll leave this when I'm satisfied I'm wrong, or when—by some miracle—it turns out that I'm right."

"But—"

"Go and present my apologies, and leave me alone!"

She bit her lip, hesitated as though about to speak again and finally complied.

The discussion did not go well. There was a feeling of resentment in the air, and even the best-intentioned proposals were liable to be met with irritable, trivial objections. It was as though everyone wanted to vent his or her anger on the people back home who had let them down, and willy-nilly the pent-up anger was overflowing onto people who could not possibly be held to blame.

And the absence of Ian was an extra straw on the camel's back of the meeting; more than once, someone muttered a rude comment and received bitter nods of agreement.

By noon, when Rorschach decreed a break for refreshment, absolutely nothing had been achieved except that grave offence had been given by Sue Tennant to Nadine Shah, by Olaf Mukerji to Karen Vlady, and by Achmed Hossein to Lucas Wong—all by perfect inadvertence, simply as the result of friction arising during the course of an argument.

Cathy trembled. This augured badly for the future of mankind on this planet. . . .

Where's Ian? If only he hadn't refused to join in, if only he'd shown common politeness, things would have gone so much more smoothly—

And at that very moment, when the company was rising and dispersing, the door was flung open and Ian appeared, striding in with clenched fists and shouting exuberantly.

"I found out what happened to the Draconians!"

There was a total, stunned silence. And then, with a hint of renewed hope, as though this at least might lighten the dismal mood of the meeting, Rorschach snapped, "Tell us!"

Ian was grinning like a fool, almost unable to prevent himself from jigging up and down.

"They went broke! They went broke! They went *bankrupt!*"

XXII

"But that's absurd," Lucas said after a pause. "Going bankrupt—well, it could bring down a civilisation, but it couldn't wipe out an entire species."

"It could!" Ian insisted. "Look, it occurred to us to wonder whether the Draconians traded among themselves, and we decided yes, they must have, but it never occurred to any of us to ask what kind of currency they employed."

Cathy jumped to her feet. "The printed crystals!" she burst out.

"Those can't have been money!" Karen shouted. "You'd find money all over everywhere, not concentrated in great big store-houses—"

"Ingots!" Sue cut in. "Gold ingots, piled up like at Fort Knox, not the actual money but the thing they used to support its value—"

"No, no, *no!*" Ian exclaimed. "Look, somebody get me a beer or something because it's going to take awhile to explain, and then I'll show you just how wrong Lucas was to say going broke couldn't kill a whole intelligent race."

"What grounds do you have—?" Achmed began, and he too was interrupted.

"The machines agree with me," Ian declared. "It all fits, every last little bit."

Igor gave a gentle cough. "I think it might be a good idea if we all got ourselves something to drink, and relaxed a little . . . don't you? I'm sure Ian knows what he's talking about, but right now he's a bit too worked up to make himself clear. Which isn't entirely surprising, hm?"

Ten minutes later, in a calmer atmosphere, Ian set aside his glass of beer and leaned back in an easy chair, crossing his legs.

"This is what I was so close to at Ash," he said. "I'd been struggling for a month to get to grips with the life pattern of an intelligent species that changed sex from active juvenile male to relatively inactive fertile female. The functional-female stage is shorter than the male stage in the contemporary species, right?" With a glance at Nadine, who nodded. "And it's followed by an infertile senile stage."

He hesitated. Impatient, Achmed said, "Well, go on!"

"I'm trying to figure out the best order to present the argument in. . . . Okay, tackle it this way. What could any given individual accumulate during the active stage that might correspond to wealth, in our terms?"

Olaf whistled loudly. "Hey! Ian, was I right when I said that what we've been calling libraries might be official data stores? Are those crystals genetic records?"

"Full marks!" Ian was still sounding slightly manic. "No wonder they appear virtually identical after this long a time—each codes not the personality of an individual, but simply his heritage. Remember at one point we were wondering whether they were indeed repositories of individual experience, records of the dead genuises whom anyone might go and consult?"

"Only the capacity wasn't adequate," Ruggiero said, leaning forward with intent concentration.

"Exactly. And we know, thanks to Nadine's work, that the na-. tives definitely practised selective breeding of both plants and animals from a very early stage in their history. We can safely hypothesise that given the senses they possessed they may have had an almost instinctive grasp of the principles of eugenics."

"They bred themselves into intelligence," Rorschach whispered.

"That's it. I owe that particular insight to Cathy. She once asked me whether the Draconians would have fallen in love. I said I doubted it. Today I woke up realising why not. If, right from the start of their incredibly rapid ascent towards a technological civilisation, they were aware that they could breed for enhanced intelligence, then they must have selected for rationality that took no

account of absurd preferences like 'love.' We had a clue right under
our noses in the fact that their expansion was calculated from the
beginning, as though planned by a machine instead of a living creature. And their population increased at a relatively slow rate, too."

"One of each!" Igor said with a chuckle.

"Yes, correct. They must have attained a degree of rationality we
can barely imagine."

"They sound terribly cold-blooded," Cathy said, and shuddered.

"No doubt we would have struck them as being intolerably tem-
peramental," Ian countered. "They'd have marvelled at the fact
that we took seven thousand years from the Neolithic stage to the
epoch of spaceflight, where they took at most half that time."

"Am I being obtuse?" Karen said. "Or have you not yet explained
how going bankrupt killed them off?"

"I was just coming to the details of that. I think I already said—
excuse me, but my head is buzzing insanely with all the implications—I think I said I started asking what an individual could accumulate by way of reward, or payment."

There was a brief hush. Nadine ventured, "Promises that when
he became she, there would be outstanding genetic lines reserved
to—uh—to her?"

"That's it. That's what killed them."

Igor leapt to his feet and started pacing back and forth, thumping
fist into palm.

"I've almost got it," he said. "You mean that without realising
what they were doing, they restricted their genetic pool until it became dangerous, and then it was too late. Like fortunes being concentrated in the hands of a few ultra-powerful families? A sort of
genetic capitalism?"

"That's a beautiful way of expressing it," Ian concurred.

"Just a second!" Sue Tennant bridled. "I don't see how they could
have reached a point of no return by that means."

"No?" Ian blinked at her. "I'm surprised. It's one of the respects
in which their thinking must have most closely paralleled our own.
They too suffered from the besetting sin of greed. How often have
human beings acted against their own best interests, and particularly on behalf of some small group rather than in favour of the race

as a whole? Our history is littered with that type of stupidity. Rational or not, the Draconians could all too easily have fallen into a similar trap. Our doom—if it overtakes us—is likely to stem from the territorial impulse, buried deep in the subconscious; someday somebody may lose control of his better judgment and initiate a war that could destroy civilisation. Anybody want to disagree?"

Two or three people murmured something to the effect that it could well have happened already: witness the failure of the *Stellaris* to return.

"On the other hand," Rorschach said, his bald-high forehead wrinkled with immense concentration, "you're saying the Draconians doomed themselves because each individual wanted to conclude *his* life—I mean life in the male stage—by racking up prospective fathers for *her* young who belonged to the finest possible strains."

"With the result that the offspring would be more intelligent on the purely rational level, in other words would have a higher IQ as we'd term it, but would not necessarily be better fitted to survive in the absolute sense. Like overbreeding a line of show dogs until they become snappy, neurotic and in the end infertile." Triumphant, Ian reached for his beer again.

"But how does all this fit in with the—I guess we have to stop calling them libraries?" Cathy said. "And the temples, too . . . though I suppose that's also a misnomer."

"Mm-hm." Wiping his upper lip, Ian nodded. "Not temples. Banks."

"What?"—from several people.

"On top: four *identical* statues, idealised, even down to the perfect regularity of their skin patterns. Below: a few pitiable crippled corpses, surrounded by such primitive artefacts it's almost incredible, down to a kind of sled that lacked even a wheel to roll it on. A symbol of ultimate riches lording it over the reality."

"Hey, that makes sense!" Olaf said softly. "All four grandparents of the finest known stock: the best-looking, the most intelligent, the most desirable. . . . Ian, I'm sold. You say you checked this out with the machines?"

Ian nodded.

"Did they produce any—ah—footnotes to what you've been saying?"

"Hell, they were still printing out when I came over here!" Ian answered. "Lord knows how long it will continue. But as soon as the point appeared to have been made, I couldn't wait to share the news with you all."

He beamed around in sheer delight.

Igor halted his pacing back and forth and resumed his chair. He said, "I think I can add one footnote straight away. We've been thinking in terms of the telescope on the moon as the climax of their achievement. They wouldn't have looked at it that way, though, would they?"

"What else, then?" Ruggiero demanded. "Something we haven't found yet?"

"No, the four statues. You yourself worked out how clever they were, how advanced a technique must have been used to give them their special finish. Wouldn't we regard somebody who devised an intelligent machine as having added more to the sum of our knowledge, in the absolute sense, than even the people who discovered the qua-space drive?" He glanced around. "No? Maybe not; I guess our bias in favour of adventure and exploration is pretty strong. But I can see it happening to the Draconians."

"I still have reservations," Lucas said, frowning. "I mean, they must have known that there were deleterious genes in their heredity, which were liable to interact and produce deformed offspring."

"Equally," Olaf said, "we know there are fatal weaknesses in the human personality which could at any moment make it unsafe to trust people with weapons of mass destruction. That hasn't prevented us building and deploying the weapons, has it?"

"What's more," Karen said, "I could imagine Draconians marvelling, on this basis, that we should still have famine on Earth so long after we invented the food converter! That can't be called rational, can it?"

"No, that's true," Lucas conceded. "Okay: for the moment I'm happy to accept Ian's theory. It's certainly the best we've ever hit on, and it does seem to make a coherent pattern out of the Draconians' entire evolution."

"Wouldn't they have realised before it was too late, though?" Nadine persisted. "How was it they didn't have time to do anything?"

"Maybe they did have time," Ian said. "And chose not to."

"But you said they were far more rational than we are!"

"And Cathy said they were cold-blooded, and Igor, right back when he was first explaining the situation to Ordoñez-Vico, mentioned the possibility of an ideology like Nazism. For all we can tell, they elevated eugenic principles to the status of a never-to-be-questioned absolute; after all, if it took them from mud huts to the moon in three thousand years, as it were, it would be dreadfully hard to discard it in a generation or two." Ian emptied his beer glass.

"On this basis," Ruggiero said, "the printed crystals are more than just—oh—birth certificates!"

"Of course. No doubt each included reference to the credit commitments obtaining at any given time. Standing to the account of Individual X, who's just entering the neuter stage, are the following items of credit: fifty with genetic line A, ten with line B, two with line C . . . and so on. Perhaps if line A is regarded as inferior to line C, Mr.-about-to-be-Mrs. X would trade twenty-five holdings in A against an extra holding in C. Oh, there are countless implications to be worked out, but—well, there's the first rough sketch."

"Ah, this is marvelous!" Igor said, rubbing his hands. "This time we're really going to have good news to send to Earth! Ian, I remember Rudolf Weil saying—"

He broke off. Everybody else was staring at him, their eyes cold.

"I think," Rorschach said in a creaking voice, "we ought to go and have lunch as we'd intended to when Ian arrived."

There were nods, and the company dispersed to the food machines.

There were so many more questions to be asked, to round out Ian's theory, that it was not until late in the evening that Cathy was able to corner him alone and hug and kiss him and eventually bury her face against his shoulder and shed a few long-restrained tears.

"Ian, I'm ashamed of not believing you," she whispered.

"What?"

"I mean, of not having believed you. Not having believed you could do it. I think you're wonderful, amazing, fantastic!"

"I'm feeling pretty pleased with myself," he admitted, one hand gently stroking her hair. "Or at any rate I was. Now . . . Oh, darling, wouldn't it be ironical if *Stellaris* never came back?"

"That's what I'm thinking about," she said. "And—yes, ironical is the word. One of the great intellectual achievements of all time, the recovery from a few scraps and shards and corpses of the facts behind the death of a whole intelligent race . . . and the only people ever to know about it would be us!"

"It's too soon to stop hoping for the ship," Ian said.

"Are you sure?"

He didn't answer.

And the ship didn't come.

XXIII

It was on the anniversary of the date when *Stellaris* ought to have returned that Valentine Rorschach committed suicide alone in his office, by plunging a knife into his throat.

Some little adjustment had been made to the facts of the future. A settlement had been planned on the most hospitable coast of the island; a survey had been carried out to determine which, if any, of the native plants could be eaten as they were by human beings, raw or plainly cooked instead of being put through the food converters; a genetic map had been constructed by Lucas, showing the optimum pattern in which they could exploit their heredity . . . but it was all of the nature of a game, or strictly a pastime. Of course there were lots of things to do. Nobody especially wanted to do them. Not now that Ian's solution to the mystery of the natives had been tested over and over without a flaw being found. It had even been reinforced by the discovery that some of the species suspected of having been modified by the Draconians were themselves genetically underfunded, as it were, and were showing above-average susceptibility to disease combined with below-average fecundity.

So there was little intellectual stimulation to be had. And Rorschach had developed cancer of the bowel.

After the funeral, a simple ceremony conducted by Lucas, Cathy said to Ian, "Something must be done! Someone's got to set an example! And it has to be you!"

Ian shook his head. "No, I'm not fit to be in charge. I'm not a leader. My heart wouldn't be in it."

"If not you, who?" She glanced around to make sure they were not in earshot of anybody else, and swung to confront him, clutching at his arm. "Ian, we can't just—just coast into oblivion, for pity's sake! We must take some positive step!"

"What?"

"Start our baby."

It had been put off, and put off. . . . He thought about it for a long while. A freak gust brought salt spray from the rocky shore of the island, tossed high over the plateau, and made him blink.

"Do you really want to?"

"I don't know what else can be done to stop us dying of sheer apathy."

"You said you wanted the first to be Igor's."

"I don't have any right to insist."

"It would be a sane decision. If we must start over on this planet, try to build something where even the natives failed . . . yes, we must always try to make sane decisions, whether or not it hurts. Find out if Igor agrees. And—Cathy!"

"Yes?"

"A question you haven't asked, but you must be wondering. I'll answer it in advance. Yes, I'll love it. Because it's yours."

She was weeping a second later when she embraced him.

"Cancer, I'm afraid," Lucas said reluctantly as Igor resumed his clothes in the biomedical office. "I imagine you already suspected that, and would rather be told bluntly than fobbed off with double-talk."

Igor nodded. "Of course. It stands to reason that where there are few infections we can even fall sick from, but where the air is always full of alien spores and germs, cancer is bound to be a common cause of death. We didn't need Valentine's death or your specialist knowledge to make that plain." He briskened. "Can it be staved off for a while?"

"Probably for years, even without surgery. But it may become very painful. The lung is a bad site." Lucas hesitated. "Thank you for taking it so well. I wish some other people could treat trivial problems equally calmly."

"It's easy to face a big problem calmly," Igor countered. "The big ones are simple, easy to define. The little ones that won't quite come into focus are what make people irritable and quarrelsome. They know something's wrong and yet they can't quite pin it down."

"There was an American phrase for that kind of talk," Lucas said with a wry smile. "They used to call it cracker-barrel philosophy."

"I notice you use the past tense," Igor said.

Lucas spread his hands. "So far as we're concerned, the whole planet Earth belongs to the past, doesn't it . . . ? By the way, something you didn't mention: did you come for examination because you'd detected symptoms?"

"Not exactly. It's because Cathy wants to start a child with me. Will it be safe?"

Lucas bit his lip. "Good, I'm glad somebody is still capable of doing more than drift along from day to day. Yes, safe insofar as heredity is concerned. As to the risk of the kid dying in infancy . . ."

"We've got to find out, or there will be two extinct intelligent races here."

"Exactly. Congratulations, Igor; Cathy has admirable good sense."

It was as though the community buckled to, summoned its collective energy, recovered the will to live. Some deep symbolic chord had been struck that resonated in their minds. Instead of talking about the new settlement, they began to build it; instead of analysing the native plants, they took the chance of eating small quantities of the most promising, and suffered nothing worse than a bout of nausea; instead of playing around with genetic lines, they seriously studied them and very shortly Sue and Olaf followed Cathy's example. Lucas recommended holding it at that level for the first year; two babies would be enough to cope with at the start.

It was a start, though. It was convincing.

"I think we're going to pull through," Cathy said softly to Ian as they stood on the headland which overlooked the site of the permanent settlement: a sheltered bay, surrounded by lush plants, that in themselves made the vista attractive if only by contrast with the starkness of the base on its disc of glass in the middle of a desert.

"So do I," Ian concurred, squeezing her hand. "Lucas says the extra oxygen down there, nearer sea level, may even be good for the kid. They give hyperbaric oxygen therapy on Earth if you can pay for it; here it comes as a built-in bonus."

"It isn't quite the way I imagined I was going to start my family," Cathy said. "To be candid, I'm not sure how I did imagine I'd do that, or even whether I was going to at all."

"You would have. Sooner or later."

"I guess so. . . ." With her eyes she was following the machines, directed by Karen, that were trenching the ground so that piping could be laid for water and sewage. "Even if we are starting under some kinds of handicap," she went on, "there are other ways in which we've got the advantage, aren't there?"

"Right. We have all the resources of a world for the taking; we don't have to pay for anything. When we get our little village ready, it'll be the most luxurious tribal settlement ever built." He chuckled. "Taking off from there, we ought to be able to work wonders in the days to come."

"Ought to . . ." Cathy echoed, and for no apparent reason had to repress a shiver. "Come on, let's go down. I'm getting chilly."

Ian stared at her blankly. "But it's so warm up here, I could— oh, no! Cathy, we go find Lucas right away!"

But there was nothing wrong with her: just a transient fluctuation of body temperature connected with pregnancy. Ian breathed again.

The tensions between them eased, faded, vanished. One could sense them dwindling from day to day. Perhaps it was because for the first time a human pattern was being lastingly imprinted on this alien world: not merely the transients' accommodation in the buildings at the base or the digs, but houses, homes, designed for occupation and family life. Perhaps it was because human beings are not satisfied with the mere awareness of intellectual achievement, but want to see, touch, admire solid testimony to the invested effort. At any rate, as the weeks passed, more and more of them took to doing things by hard physical labour which might have been done in half the time by their machines: dragging rocks into position to make foundations, erecting poles, laying floors of sand—to be fused into glass with a carefully focussed solar-furnace beam—and taking pride in making them flat with no more help than a straightedge and a level.

"I never realised just how much I knew about making things," Igor commented happily to Ian one day.

"I hope you passed the talent on," Ian answered with a chuckle. "It's going to be needed!"

The day the settlement was ready for living in, they held a party: a grand celebration of the kind that they had hoped to hold when the ship next came back . . . but nobody was tactless enough to refer to that. There was music, and this time it wasn't all from tapes, because Olaf had found a native plant—perhaps modified by the Draconians for some unknown reason—whose tubular stems were of uniform size and near-uniform length, out of which he had made six-hole pipes on the Indian pattern. Handing these out, he instructed the company to close and open certain holes in turn while Sue beat on a little drum she had made from a kind of shell found on the beach covered with the ballonet skin of one of what they were now casually calling "birds" even if they were more like aerial jellyfish. Unexpectedly they realised they were playing nursery-rhyme tunes in three-part harmony.

There was dancing, too, and there were stupid childish games that made them laugh inordinately, and there were stale but funny stories, the older the better as though they wanted to reach back into the past before it escaped them altogether behind a barrier as impermeable as qua-space to a naked man.

And there was a special treat when it came time to eat supper: a dish for each of them except Sue and Cathy of the first native plant proved to be completely edible. The machines said it was, and turn and turn about volunteers had confirmed the assumption, starting with a mouthful, then taking a handful and finally making a complete meal. It was a kind of seedpod, the colour of an egg-plant and the shape of a pear, and it tasted—well, it tasted vaguely . . . It . . .

It was an *acquired* taste, Igor said in an exaggeratedly judicious tone, and they clapped the exactness of his description. Nonethe-less, it was delicious, as being the first sign that one day a man might walk this world without the aid of complicated machines.

All in all it was a perfectly wonderful party, and when eventually they grew so tired they had to make for bed, they were still chuck-ling, and a few of the most energetic danced to the accompaniment of their own whistling as they dispersed into their new beautiful cottagelike homes.

The following morning Lucas Wong did not wake up. Follow-ing computerised instructions, Nadine performed an autopsy on him, and discovered he had been killed by a cerebral hemorrhage. A weak-walled artery had burst.

All their newfound hope evaporated; it was instantly as though the euphoria of the past months had been a dream, and suddenly they had been rudely aroused.

It was useless to remind themselves that this could have hap-pened at any time, and that the fact was proved by the medical computer store; dutifully, Lucas had conducted a routine examina-tion of himself at the same intervals as he checked out everybody else, and last time he had realised he was suffering from acute hypertension and one of his leg veins had varicosed . . . in respect of which he had taken the proper medication.

No, those qualifications were at most palliative. What hurt was that the doctor was dead. Even Cathy, who sometimes seemed to Ian the most level-headed of them all, woke crying in the night from bad dreams in which because there was no Lucas to deliver her baby it came into the world deformed and imbecilic, whereas if he'd survived he could, as though by magic, have ensured that the child was tall and beautiful and brilliant.

It was a time for looking up data in the medical computer store concerning postpartum depression and even maternal schizophrenia . . . only to discover that the authorities back on Earth had never for one moment believed such information might be necessary. There was neither help nor guidance on the files.

The baby was absolutely normal when she was born: a girl weighing just over three kilos, with hair that she lost a day or two later and then regrew.

She lived to be exactly—to the hour—one month old. Sue's baby, a boy, was premature, and survived a mere eleven days.

XXIV

"Is there a Creator who is jealous of intelligence? Looking at thirty-two graves, I could believe it. Feeling this unspeakable loneliness, I could imagine that I'm hated because I did what was forbidden: fathomed a mystery that was never meant to be solved. . . ."

But that was maudlin rambling, and these writing materials were too precious to waste. Bleary-eyed, seated at a table made from a salvaged scrap of aluminium, shivering so much his hand threatened to distort the words he was inscribing with acid dye on other and yet other plates of metal, Ian groaned. It had taken him a long time to work out how he might leave a message on something more durable than paper or magnetic tape.

This idea had come to him when he was setting up an improvised headstone over a new grave.

Achmed's, I think, or was it Ruggiero's . . . ? Does it matter?

Even now the suspicion haunted him that he had chosen the less-than-best means; metal too could be corroded, these slow awkward words could be dissolved much as they had been etched. . . . But he was in great pain, and what little concentration he could summon might better be applied to leaving a blurred message than none at all. He gathered his forces and continued.

. . . thirty-two graves. No, we didn't start another baby after the shock and horror of losing first Cathy's, then Sue's. One of those graves, complete with a marker, is for me. I've been sleeping in it since I recovered enough from my last illness to move about and do things like digging and writing.

I think I've gone insane. In fact I'm sure I have. But I'm not surprised. I've been alone for a long time now. At the end there were four of us. I mean I wasn't the one who lasted longest, not really, because I just collapsed one day—the world started to swim around me and Olaf said I had a five-degree fever and found me some place to lie down and brought me some sort of medicine. . . . I'd started to believe that the food converters weren't working any longer when you switched them to the drug mode. I mean so many people had died even with what was supposed to be the best medicine. And I guess I was wrong because I got better—well, a few days later I could get up and find something to drink, just a puddle of rainwater but I was terribly thirsty, and . . .

Well, there they were. The others. Dead as mutton. The last and toughest except me: Olaf, and Achmed, and Ruggiero. Funny; we thought the women were going to be the toughest, same as back on Earth. Only, you see, Cathy killed herself, and so did Sue, and Karen got in this lunatic fight with Achmed that time when Achmed was delirious and was so terrified of dying without a son—some kind of Muslim hangup—and she lost such a lot of blood she . . .

Never mind. I put what I could think of to say about them on the gravestones. Grave markers. Whatever.

And of course the way they died was the thing I was most aware of. Like the babies. I had to do the autopsies on both of them. Weird. Nadine should have done them, same as for Lucas, but somehow she said she couldn't face it, and I . . . Well, maybe I was just the person who wanted to know the answer that much more than anybody else did. I cut them up. Like a butcher. Had nightmares for years afterwards. I still do. I think it's been years. Keep seeing in my dreams the way the internal organs spilled out on the big sterile table. If I get reincarnated next time, I want to be a vegetarian, a Hindu or something, and very orthodox. I want to forget that, except I can't when I'm asleep.

I got to stop wasting this ink stuff!

Starting over, next day. I was going to explain about the babies. In their lungs we found a kind of puffy fungus thing. We got it all worked out. An aerophytic plant, an equivalent to the orchids you find on Earth. But instead of landing in full view on the trunk of a tree, or a branch or whatever, it starts its life cycle in some dark warm crevice where there's plenty of moisture. It's only the size of a yeast spore when it drifts around looking for a place to start growing, and it's sort of delicate until it gets a proper grip on life. In the lungs of an adult, it simply drowns in the regular phlegmy secretions. All of us must have breathed in spores like that and just coughed them up again. The babies couldn't. I wish I didn't keep wondering about poor Igor and the cancer he had in his lungs. I'm sure it could have started from almost any cause even if he didn't ever smoke cigarettes. I mean back on Earth if he breathed the exhaust from an unfiltered car or something. But he died in such agony and he took so long about it and nobody deserved that much suffering, nobody, not even a mass murderer, and Igor was the kindest and gentlest person in the world! I mean both worlds. I hated watching him die. I guess if I am crazy that was when it started. I know it was his loss that kicked Cathy over the edge, not just the kid's death but his, too. I think I already put it down some place that he was—oh, on the grave marker. I keep on mentioning grave markers but that's what I see most of when I look up. I'm sitting facing them so when I forget what I ought to be saying I can look up and remember, oh of course, we had somebody called Valentine Rorschach who was the director, and we had Lucas Wong who was the doctor and chief biologist, and the rest of the people I wish were here to keep me company!

Rereading what I managed to write yesterday, and feeling today a lot better than I've felt for ages—not sweating or shaking nearly so much—I realise I'm wasting time and ink. I'm talking about things that could be pieced together from other sources. But I guess I should write down what we found out here, because the other night—I think—I saw an electrical storm up there on the plateau where we left the base, and a lightning strike could play merry hell with the computer memories, hm? Down here at the settlement, where we shouldn't have moved to because if we'd stayed up in that dry dusty air those babies wouldn't have inhaled spores and suffocated—but maybe they would, who can say? Forget it. They're dead.

Yes, anyway. We found out that the Draconians inbred to the point of simple genetic collapse because they used commitment to fertilise each other as the basis for their medium of exchange. In other words, they counted their fortune according to the excellence of the genetic lines that would father their children when they shifted into the female stage. Within a very short time—about a thousand generations—they had so depleted their gene pool that they lost their immunity to some disease, or some recessive gene became endemic, or both or more than that. Never mind. They're dead, too. And they brought their doom on themselves, I'm certain of that. In fact it was among the first clues I had to their capacity for being stupid even if they were brilliant. Oh, they were so like us in their faults! I can even imagine we might have become friends if our time in the universe had overlapped. . . . Never mind. They had all these biological skills; what would be the first use they made of them? Prolong the active-male stage, obviously. That was when things really got done.

On top of which they wanted to be fertilised, when they turned female, from *only* the best lines. The longer they could postpone the day of reckoning, the better chance they had of accumulating good commitments: maybe not from the original person making the contract, but from his/her offspring, or siblings, or kinfolk. So it would have been desirable to breed for a short female stage. In the end they overdid it. There were only females with short fertile periods, capable of having one or two offspring, but jealously guarding the right to be fecundated because they'd spent their active lives investing in it. No doubt they had regulations to punish males who fertilised females they were not under contract to. And enforced the regulations brutally. I don't know. I'm not as well as I thought. I'm not sure if I got that right or whether it refers to Earth.

I wish I hadn't put down "Earth" in the last line I wrote yesterday. I've been struggling not to think about Earth. I keep having this other crazy dream—I think I said something about one of the dreams I get but this one is different—where I wake up in the morning and there's *Stellaris* coming down and everybody turns out to greet her and I see Valentine and Cathy and Igor and everybody and we're all waiting there until the air lock opens and then out comes Colonel Weil all beaming and cheerful and I remember he's been retired and I look around and it isn't my friends who are standing with me to welcome the ship.

It's Draconians. Thousands of them. All as huge as the statues we found at Peat. They loom over me and pay no attention to my existence, just walk into the ship one after another and the lock closes behind them and off they go, to somewhere—I don't know—and there I am, alone, in the middle of the plateau and there aren't even any buildings.

When I have that dream, I wake up with my throat so sore I guess I must have been screaming for a long time. Just as well there isn't anybody to hear me.

I was going to face thinking about Earth, only yesterday I got very sick again. I've been passing blood. I don't expect I have much longer to go.

It gets very hard to drag metal plates here to write on and making this acid ink seems to be doing wrong things to the food converters, I mean it was supposed to be okay to reset them to make practically anything just synthesising from the available elements but having stuff that will bite into metal may be doing something to the innards. . . . Oh, I don't know. Just keep on as long as I can. It distracts me. Speaking of something being done to innards, I brought up my breakfast today. Thought it was kind of odd when I ate it. But I don't have the skills to make tests and analyse the food and whatever.

I got this bruise on my arm. Taking a terrible time to go away.

Earth. Yes. I vaguely recall the place. And of course the whole reason I'm writing this down is because I'm sure they're going to send the ship back soon, or another ship in a hundred years' time maybe, and I want somebody to be able to find out what happened here, obviously not just to the Draconians but to us, too, in case they get all sorts of wrong ideas like it's not legal to go to another star. Riridu—ridiculous! (Mustn't make spelling mistakes because of wasint ink.)

Look, it isn't like that at all! Sure, the Draconians failed because of what they bred out of themselves—must have done. Discounted the importance of things that had enabled them to evolve from the brute because they were so high on the idea of being able to reason they didn't worry about losing immunities and such so long as they were able to look better and think better and invent more ingenious gadgets. I can hear them arguing in my head sometimes: so what does it matter if they have an underdeveloped glotch in that family? We didn't hear of a death from glotchitis in umpty-dozen seasons, did we?

Or words to that effect. No, I don't mean words. I mean. What I mean *is*, it was what they bred out of themselves that they tripped over. With us, my best guess from nineteen light-years away is that what did for us was what we didn't breed into ourselves. Like compassion, and generosity, and love.

You know, I'd rather this message never got read than that it was picked up by somebody on the winning side in a war that wiped out half mankind. I just wouldn't want people that dangerous to go roaming around the galaxy. I'd be ashamed to have my race remembered and recognised as vicious killers. All of a sudden my mind is very lucid. I think that's a bad sign. I recall how Nadine became very articulate and forceful just a few hours before she died, and so did Igor in spite of being doped to the eyeballs. I feel slightly cold, but very much in control. I ought to be hungry, but I have no appetite. The bruise on my arm is bright purple, as though new red blood is leaking from the capillaries just under the skin.

And that's not the only place. I just realised I have a sweetish taste in my mouth. My gums are bleeding.

Oh well.

You know, I often wondered about being aware of death. It isn't too bad. Not compared with what the Draconians went through, knowing they were going to become extinct. For all I can tell, right this minute the *Stellaris* may be broadcasting frantic signals, trying to make us answer. I don't particularly want to go and look, though. I'm tired. I'm very old. Being alone makes one feel old. I wish I didn't have one more thing I want to say that I can't quite remember, because it's important and I have to carry on until I do recall it in case I break off and find I can't start again— Got it.

I was going to say this. We mustn't MUST NOT let the pattern spread. We mustn't quit, mustn't give up, mustn't act in such a fashion that when one day some species on some other planet goes looking for friends all that can be found is ruins and corpses and fossils. Right here we figured out why the Draconians didn't make it—don't say "Ian Macauley figured it out," say always THEY figured it out, human beings, a whole bunch working together. Make kids excited about that, make them admire it, make them want to do the same sort of thing! But never let them forget that just thinking isn't enough. You can become arrogant by thinking, you can imagine you know it all and there are always things you don't know that can wreck your hopes and smash your dreams.

I meant to say something else. I'm so cold, though. I keep yawning and blood trickles out of my mouth when I open it. I want to go and join Cathy. I love her very much and I never had time to tell her so the way I wanted to. So I guess I –